I0661132

Daniel Wise

**Jessie Carlton**

The Story of a Girl who Fought with the Little Impulse, the Wizard, and Conquered

him.

Daniel Wise

**Jessie Carlton**
*The Story of a Girl who Fought with the Little Impulse, the Wizard, and Conquered him.*

ISBN/EAN: 9783744749572

Printed in Europe, USA, Canada, Australia, Japan

Cover: Foto ©Andreas Hilbeck / pixelio.de

More available books at **www.hansebooks.com**

# GLEN MORRIS STORIES.

# JESSIE CARLTON;

## THE STORY OF

# A GIRL WHO FOUGHT WITH LITTLE IMPULSE, THE WIZARD, AND CONQUERED HIM.

### By FRANCIS FORRESTER, Esq.

(DANIEL WISE, D.D.,)

AUTHOR OF "BOY TRAVELERS IN ARABIA," "YOUNG KNIGHTS OF THE CROSS," "SOME REMARKABLE WOMEN," "MEN OF RENOWN," "OUR MISSIONARY HEROES AND HEROINES," "LINDENDALE STORIES," "SKETCHES AND ANECDOTES OF AMERICAN METHODISTS," "HEROIC METHODISTS OF THE OLDEN TIME," "YOUNG MAN'S COUNSELOR," "YOUNG LADIES' COUNSELOR," "PATH OF LIFE," "PLEASANT PATHWAYS," "SQUIRE OF WALTON HALL," ETC., ETC.

NEW YORK: PHILLIPS & HUNT.
CINCINNATI: CRANSTON & STOWE.
1888.

JESSIE TALKING TO ROVER.

Front.

# NOTE

TO PARENTS, GUARDIANS, AND TEACHERS.

———

The purpose of the "GLEN MORRIS STORIES" is to sow the seed of pure, noble, manly character in the mind of our grent nation's childhood. They exhibit the virtues and vices of childhood, not in prosy, uu·readable precepts, but in a series of characters which move before the imagination as living beings do before the senses. Thus access to the heart is won by way of the imagination. While the story charms, the truth sows itself in the conscience and in the affections. The child is thereby led to abhor the false and the vile, and to sympathize with the right, the beautiful, and the true. To every parent, teacher, and guardian, who has affinity with these high purposes, the "Glen Morris Stories" are most respectfully inscribed by their fellow·laborer in the field of childhood.

FRANCIS FORRESTER.

# ORDER OF THE GLEN MORRIS STORIES.

I. Guy Carlton, the Story of a Boy who belonged to the "Try Company."

II. Dick Duncan, the Story of a Boy who loved Mischief.

III. Jessie Carlton, the Story of a Girl who fought with little Impulse, the Wizard, and conquered him.

IV. Walter Sherwood, the Story of an easy, good-natured Boy.

V. Kate Carlton, the Story of a vain Girl.

# CONTENTS.

CHAPTER                                         PAGE

I.—JESSIE AND THE WIZARD............................ 11

II.—JESSIE'S TWO COUSINS.............................. 27

III—A NUTTING-PARTY................................. 43

IV.—JESSIE'S GREAT SORROW........................... 61

V.—THE BROKEN MIRROR............................. 78

VI.—THE FIRST SLIDE OF THE SEASON.................. 94

VII.—JESSIE'S FIRST GREAT VICTORY.................... 112

VIII.—FAREWELL TO THE COUSINS....................... 126

IX.—THE WIZARD IN THE FIELD AGAIN................ 140

X.—MADGE CLIFTON................................. 157

XI.—MADGE CLIFTON'S MOTHER....................... 172

XII.—LITTLE IMPULSE BEATEN AGAIN................... 186

XIII.—THE SKATING-PARTY............................. 200

XIV.—THE WATCH-POCKET FINISHED ................... 215

XV.—THANKSGIVING DAY.............................. 231

# ENGRAVINGS.

Jessie talking to Rover—*Frontispiece.*

Illustrated Title-page.

Jessie and Emily sailing Boats in the Quarry......Page 51

Jessie and Carrie enjoying a Slide................... " 105

Mrs. Moneypenny reading Jack's Letter............ " 153

Guy Coasting with Jessie......................... " 227

## PRINCIPAL CHARACTERS IN THIS STORY.

Jessie Carlton, only daughter of a New York merchant residing at Glen Morris Cottage, Duncanville, a village near New York.

Emily and Charlie Morris, Jessie's two cousins, visiting at Glen Morris Cottage.

Madge Clifton, Jessie's *protégé.*

Carrie Sherwood, one of Jessie's companions.

Mrs. Moneypenny, a poor widow, and her son Jack

# JESSIE CARLTON.

## CHAPTER I.

### JESSIE AND IMPULSE THE WIZARD.

ON a bright afternoon of a warm day in October, JESSIE CARLTON sat in the parlor of Glen Morris Cottage. Her elbows rested on the table, her face was held between her two plump little hands, and her eyes were feasting on some charming pictures which were spread out before her. A pretty little work-basket stood on a chair at her side. It contained several yards of rumpled patchwork, two pieces of broadcloth with figures partially worked on them as if they were intended for a pair of slippers, a watch-pocket half finished, and a small piece of silk composed of very little squares.

On the table close to her left elbow was a cam
bric handkerchief with some embroidery jus(
begun in one of its corners. A needle carelessly stuck into it showed that Jessie had been
working on it when her eyes were attracted by
the pictures she was now studying with such
close attention.

After a few minutes the little girl moved her
right arm for the purpose of looking at another
picture, when her thimble dropped from her
finger to the table with a loud ringing sound.
She started to pick it up, and in so doing
pushed her scissors to the floor. The noise
they made in falling led Jessie to glance towards
the sofa, and to say in a very soft whisper—

"Oh dear! I'm afraid those naughty scissors
have waked Uncle Morris out of his nap!"

Jessie was right. The noise had started Uncle
Morris from a cozy little nap into which he had
fallen after dinner. It was not often that the
active old gentleman indulged himself in this
way; but a long walk in the morning had made
him weary, and he had quietly roamed into
dream-land as he sat reading. He now opened

his eyes, looked round the room, and seeing his niece looking askance at him, said—

"What's the matter, Jessie? I heard something fall with a great crash, what was it?"

Jessie laughed outright. It was not very polite, but she could not very well keep the fun out of her face. It seemed so queer that her uncle should call the noise made by the fall of a pair of scissors *a great crash*. At last she said—

"There was no great crash, Uncle. Only my scissors fell from the table."

"Was that all? Why it sounded to me just like the crash of a tray full of crockery ware. That was because I was half asleep, I suppose. Well, never mind, I'm not the first old gentleman who has magnified a little noise into a great one in his sleep—but what are you so busy about this afternoon, little puss!"

As Uncle Morris put this question he arose, walked up to the table and began to look at Jessie's work, for by this time she had begun stitching on the cambric handkerchief again. Blushing deeply, she said—

"I am embroidering a pocket-handkerchief, Uncle."

"Indeed! how fond you little ladies are of finery !" said Uncle Morris, smiling and patting Jessie's head.

"I'm not doing it for myself, Uncle," replied the child.

"Not for yourself, eh ? Is it for papa, then ?"

"No, Sir."

" For your brother Guy, perhaps ?"

"No, Sir.  Not for Guy," and looking slyly at her uncle, she added.  " I guess that you are not Yankee enough to guess whom it is for."

" For your brother Hugh, maybe ?"

" You must guess again, Uncle."

" Well, maybe it is for your hero, Richard Duncan."

" O Uncle! Do you think I would embroider a handkerchief for a young gentleman !" and Jessie pursed up her lips as though she was go· ing to be very angry.

" Don't be angry with your old uncle, my little puss," said Mr. Morris with an air of mock penitence, " I had an idea that young

ladies did such things for young gentlemen
sometimes. But who is it for? I give it
up."

"You give it up! Why, I thought you belonged to the 'never give up company.' Oh,
fy! Uncle Morris, I'll get you turned out of tho
try company if you don't mind. So you had
better guess again," and Jessie held up her fat
finger and looked so funnily at Mr. Morris that
the old gentleman's heart warmed towards her,
and giving her a kiss of fond affection, ho
said—

"Then I guess it is for your poor old uncle."

"Beans are hot!" cried Jessie, clapping her
hands. "You've guessed it at last. But see
my work, Uncle! Isn't it beautiful?"

"Very pretty, indeed, my dear," replied the
old man, who now put on a comical look, and
added, "but I'm afraid I shall not live until it
is finished."

"Not live——!" Jessie was going to be
alarmed, but her uncle's laughing eyes checked
her alarm, and catching his meaning from his
expression, she pouted and was silent.

"Don't put on that frightful pout, my little puss, for, really, I should have to live as long a life as an ancient patriarch if I do not die before you are likely to *finish* the handkerchief. There are the quilt, the slippers, the watch-pocket, the chair-cushion, and the handkerchief all *begun* for me, but nothing finished. That little wizard—his name is Impulse, you know—which led you to drop the quilt that you might begin the slippers, and the slippers that you might begin the chair-cushion, will soon tempt you to drop the handkerchief for something else. I wish I could catch the jolly little imp. I'd cane him smartly, and then I would lead him to Parson Resolution's church, and marry him to that sweet little fairy, Miss Persever-ance, who is breaking her heart for the love of him　Were he once thus married, I think his bride would teach him to help you finish all the little gifts you have begun for me, and there would be some hope that I should live long enough to sleep under your quilt, sit on your cushion, walk in your slippers, put my watch in your pocket at night, and blow my venerable nose in your embroidered pocket handkerchief."

The reproof so pleasantly given in these quaint words found its way to Jessie's heart. Her face became sober, she bit her lips, a stray tear or two hung, like dew-drops in the web of a gossamer, on her long eyelashes, she sighed and after a few moments of silent thought rose, planted her right foot firmly on the floor, and said—

"Uncle Morris, I *will* conquer that little wizard! I WILL *finish* your quilt right away, and then all the other things in their turn—see if I don't."

Jessie had made just such a promise at least *ten* times, since Glen Morris Cottage had become her home. She had tried to keep it too, but, somehow, *her habit of yielding to every new impulse which came over her*, had hitherto led her to break it as often as it had been made. The little wizard, as Uncle Morris face- tiously called her changeful impulses, was her tyrant. The jolly little rogue did, indeed, sadly stand in need of matrimony with the forlorn

2

Miss Perseverance. For poor Jessie's sake, Uncle Morris was very anxious to see the wedding come off speedily. Whether his wish was met or not, will appear hereafter.

To prove her sincerity Jessie put the cambric handkerchief in the bottom of her work-basket. The other articles she placed, in the order in which she had begun them, above it, and then sat resolutely down to her patchwork quilt. As her bright little needle began to fly with the swiftness of a weaver's shuttle, she said to herself—

"Now I *will* finish Uncle Morris's quilt right off."

Uncle Morris had left the parlor, and Jessie had sewed steadily for at least fifteen minutes, when her brother Hugh bounded into the room, holding two letters in his hand, and said—

"Letters for Jessie Carlton and her mother. Postage one dollar, to be paid to the bearer on delivery. Give me your half-dollar, Miss Carlton, and I will give you your letter!"

"A letter for me!" cried Jessie, dropping her work and running to her brother, capsizing her work-basket as she ran. "Give it to me! Give it to me."

"Pay me the postage first," said Hugh, holding the letter over her head.

"There is no postage, you know there isn't, you naughty Hugh! Give me my letter," and Jessie pulled Hugh's arm in the vain attempt to bring the letter within her reach.

"No postage, indeed! Do you think Uncle Sam can afford to carry letters for all the Yankee girls who may choose to write to each other, without pay? Not he. Uncle Sam knows how to care for number one too well for that. So hand over your half-dollar, Miss Jessie, and I will give you your letter."

Jessie coaxed and scolded at her brother for nearly ten minutes, in vain. Hugh loved to tease her, and so he kept on, now offering the letter, and then holding it beyond her reach, until the poor child's patience being all gone, she sat down and cried with vexation. This was certainly carrying his fun too far. A little pleasant bantering at first, though not *amiable*, might have been pardonable; but now that her feelings were hurt he was very unkind to carry his nonsense any further. But this was one of Hugh's faults. He was a great tease. Seeing his sister in tears, he said, in a whining tone—

"Pretty little cry-baby !. How beautiful you are, all melted into tears !" Then dropping the whine from his tone, he added, " Here, Jessie, take your letter !"

Jessie stretched out her arm to take the offered letter. Hugh drew it back again and said—

" Bah ! Don't you wish you may get it !"

" You unamiable boy ! is that the affection which is due from a brother to his sister ? O Hugh ! Hugh ! I wish you had more love and less selfishness in that idle soul of yours."

This just rebuke from the lips of Uncle Morris, who had been standing unperceived for the last few minutes behind the half-open door, put an end to all Master Hugh's idle, not to say wicked, teasing. He dropped the letters into Jessie's lap, and with an angry scowl on his face left the room.

The sunshine came back into Jessie's face in a moment. She looked her thanks to Uncle Morris, while she nervously opened the en velope of her letter. Having unfolded it, she read as follows:

MORRISTOWN, New Jersey, October 10th. 18—

DEAR COUSIN JESSIE,

Pa and Ma have just given their consent to have me and my brother Charlie visit you at Glen Morris Cottage. I am so glad I can hardly hold my pen to write you about it. Charlie is jumping about the room, and shouting hurrah, for joy. We are to start Thursday, in the afternoon train, and shall get to your house to tea. With ten thousand kisses for you, I remain,

Your affectionate cousin,

EMILY MORRIS.

MISS JESSIE CARLTON.

"Oh, won't it be nice, Uncle Morris!" cried Jessie, after reading this note. "What good times I shall have with my cousins! I'm so glad I don't know what to do with myself."

"You are a happy little puss generally, and I am glad to see you made happier than usual by this pleasant letter from your cousin. But are you sure, my dear Jessie, that you will enjoy your cousins' visit?"

"Why, Uncle!" cried Jessie, with an air of surprise. "How can you ask me such a question? I am sure I shall love my cousins very much, and we shall enjoy ourselves very finely together."

"Well! Well! I hope it may be so," said Uncle Morris, with a sigh which made Jessie think that the good old man's hope was not a very strong one. She said nothing, however, and Uncle Morris asked—

"When are your cousins coming?"

Jessie looked at her letter and read, "'We are to start Thursday,'"—pausing, and looking up, she exclaimed—

"Why, that's this very day! I declare they will be here this afternoon. Won't it be nice!"

"Yes, to-day *is* Thursday. Your letter has been delayed. Perhaps you had better take your mamma's letter to her room. She may re-

quire time to make preparations for her young
guests. They will be here—let me see (looking
at his watch), in two hours. Run Jessie and
tell your mother!"

Jessie hurried to her mother's apartment
with the unopened letter and the news. Mrs.
Carlton's letter was from Emily's mother and
contained the same information.

Jessie was in ecstasies during the next two
hours. To be sure, there was that question
and that sigh of Uncle Morris to cast a slight
shadow on her joy. But shadows never tarried
long on Jessie's spirit, which was so bright and
joyous that it seemed as if it was made of sunshine. Happy little Jessie Carlton!

Emily's letter had put all thought of her
work out of Jessie's head. Her patchwork lay
on the floor beside the overturned work-basket,
until her mother going to prepare the parlor
for company, picked both up and put them
away In fact, Jessie's little wizard had her in
his chains again. She was once more the sim
ple-hearted child of impulse.

Having fixed her hair and changed her dress,

Jessie ran out on to the piazza to watch for the coming of her cousins. First she seated herself on the settee, which stood there, and made the air ring again with her joyous song. After a few minutes, she sprang from her seat and seizing old Rover by the head, began to tell him that her cousins were coming, and, therefore, he must be the very best behaved dog in the world.* Then seating herself lightly on old Rover's back, she patted his neck, and said—

"Noble old Rover, won't you give your mistress a ride?"

Rover was a grand old dog, large and strong enough to carry a much heavier miss than Jessie. He was good-natured too. Still he had no notion of being used for a pony. So, after standing quite still for a moment or two, he suddenly started and sent Jessie sprawling on the piazza, while he trotted down the steps and made a bed for himself in the greensward, on the lawn, as quietly as if nothing had happened. A knowing old dog was Rover.

---

* See Frontispiece.

Jessie picked herself up and began singing again. Scarcely had she trilled out two lines before she saw Guy coming towards the house. With the light spring of a fairy she bounded across the lawn, and meeting him at the gate exclaimed—

"O Guy, cousin Emily and cousin Charlie are coming here to-night. Aren't you glad?"

"To be sure I am. I'm glad of any thing that pleases my sister."

Jessie kissed him, and taking his hand, walked with him back to the piazza, where she resumed her watching, beguiling the time by humming her songs and by an occasional frolic with old Rover.

At last, the sound of wheels told her that the carriage was coming up from the railroad station. A few minutes later it rolled along the road which ran through the lawn and in front of the piazza. Four bright eyes peeped over the door, which the coachman speedily opened. Mr. Carlton stepped out first and then came Emily and Charlie. Never did cousins meet with warmer greetings than they received from

Jessie and Guy, and Mrs. Carlton. and Uncle Morris. Never was little girl happier than Jessie, when, a few minutes later, she had Emily all to herself, in her own sweet little chamber, showing her the contents of drawer and trunk and doll-house, and whatever else might be included in the term "playthings." When Emily and Charlie went to bed that night, they were in ecstasies over the pleasant things they had seen and felt on the first evening of their visit to Glen Morris Cottage.

# CHAPTER II.

THE first few days of her cousins' visit were like a pleasant dream to Jessie. She had so much to say, and so many things to show to her visitors, that they could scarcely help sharing the joy which welled up within her like a crystal stream from a mountain spring. Seeing them so cheerful and happy, Jessie wondered more and more at the question her uncle had asked her about enjoying their visit.

"I don't see what Uncle Morris meant," said she to herself one afternoon, while her cousins were on the lawn laughing and playing with Guy, and she was washing her hands by way of preparation for tea. "He looked and sighed," she went on to say, "as if he thought I should be disappointed in them. But I am not. They are the kindest, merriest cousins in the world. I declare I'll ask Uncle Morris what he meant, the next time I see him alone."

That next time came very soon, for as Jessie skipped down stairs, with laughter twinkling in her eyes, and a song tripping from her tongue, she met her uncle in the hall. Running right to him, she seized his arm, peered curiously into his face, and said—

"Uncle Morris?"

"Well, little puss, what now?" replied the old gentleman, as he kissed her rosy cheeks.

"I want you to tell me what you sighed and shook your head for, last week, when I told you what good times I was going to have with my cousins?" said Jessie, closely watching the expression of the old gentleman's face.

There was a merry twinkle in Uncle Morris's eyes, as he replied, "You have a good memory for a laughing little puss. Well, I'm glad you have not yet found out why I sighed. I hope you won't make the discovery, though I fear you will before another week passes. There is a proverb which says, *It's only the shoe that knows whether the stocking has holes in it or*

*not.* Now, Jessie, if you can find out the meaning of this proverb, you will know why I sighed.
If you dor't find it out in a week, I'll explain
it t: you."

" How funny!" exclaimed the little girl; and
then, putting on a thoughtful air, she repeated
the proverb slowly, in an undertone; after
which, she added aloud, "I don't see what
shoes and stockings have to do with my cousins
and me. What a funny man you are, Uncle
Morris!"

Uncle Morris had, by this time, reached the
door leading to the back piazza. He heard this
exclamation, however, and turning round, with
the door-knob in his hand, he peeped through
the opening, shook his forefinger at her, and
said—

" When Jessie knows her cousins as the shoe
knows the stocking, she will be able to tell
why I sighed. Ha! ha! ha! Uncle Morris is a
funny man, is he?"

Just then a loud voice was heard ringing
through the hall, and saying—

" Cousin Jessie! Cousin Jessie! come here

quick! Your ugly old dog is killing my sister!"

"Not quite so bad as that, I guess," said Jessie, when she reached the front door, where she saw Emily sitting on the green sward, rubbing the back of her head. Old Rover was standing on the piazza, uttering a low growl at Charlie, by way of warning him not to throw any more stones at his dogship.

"He's an ugly monster, that he is," said the boy, hurling another stone at Rover, as he moved toward his mistress, and began to rub his nose against her hands.

"Down, Rover!" said Jessie, patting the dog's head, and thus quieting his temper, which was somewhat ruffled by the last stone, which Charlie had sent right against his ribs.

"I *will* stone him, if I want to," growled Charlie, pouting his lips, puffing out his cheeks, and stamping his foot, as Guy laid his hand on his right arm.

"No, no, Charlie, you must not stone old Rover. It is not kind to hurt a poor, harmless dog, nor is it quite safe, either, for, you see,

Rover has big teeth, and he may bite you if you hurt him," said Guy, still holding the angry boy.

"I don't care! He hurt my sister. I'll kick you if you don't let me stone him as much as I like. Let me go, you ugly fellow!" and with these words, Charlie kicked and struggled with such violence, that Guy could scarcely hold him.

Meanwhile, Jessie, having sent old Rover to his kennel, was trying to comfort Emily. The whole difficulty had grown out of her attempt to mount the dog's back, in defiance of Guy's advice. He told her that Rover did not like to do service as a pony, and that he would certainly throw her off if she tried to ride him. But, urged on by Charlie, she had seated herself on the dog, and had been thrown down just as Jessie had been, a few days before. She was not much hurt, a slight bruise on the back of her head being the only damage she had sustained. Jessie would have laughed over such a trifle. But Emily was not like Jessie. She had been pleasant thus far, since her coming to

Glen Morris. But now, her good-nature being played out, she began to show the selfish and ugly side of her character.

"Never mind that little hurt, dear Emily," said Jessie, as she passed her hand lightly over the bruise. "If you will go into the house with me, I'll get mother to rub a little *arnica* upon it, and that will make it well very soon."

"I won't go in; and if your father don't have that ugly dog killed, I'll go home to-morrow, that I will!"

"What! have Rover killed? Oh, no! Pa won't do that, I'm sure," said Jessie, a little startled at the idea of dear old Rover's death.

"I'll kill him!" screamed Charlie, who was still a sulky prisoner in Guy's hands.

"You are a little fellow to play the part of a butcher!" said Mr. Morris, who had now come to the front of the house, and had been quietly surveying the scene, for a few moments past, from behind a large evergreen, unperceived by all but Guy.

"I'm glad you are come, Uncle," said Guy, "for I did not know what to do with this little

lump of spunk.  I guess that Jessie is glad, too,
for she seems puzzled to know what to do with
Emily, who is as sulky as Charlie here is
spunky."

The presence of Uncle Morris quieted Charlie, and made Emily rise from the grass.  But
nothing that he could say, after hearing the
whole story, could restore them to good humor.
Charlie bit his thumb, and scowled; while Emi
ly, pushing Jessie from her side, kept rolling
her pocket-handkerchief into a ball, pouted, and
refused to say a word, either to her uncle or
cousin.

In this wretched mood they went in to tea,
sitting at the table like two dark shadows falling across a room full of sunshine.  Everybody
was kind to them.  Jessie did her utmost to
restore them to good humor.  Uncle Morris
said funny things, hoping to make them smile.
But it was no use.  Smile they would not; and
when tea was over, they both slunk away to a
distant part of the room, and kept up their
sulks until bedtime.  Even then, when Jessie
tried to kiss Emily, she was rudely pushed aside.

3

"I don't want to kiss anybody in this house," muttered the ugly child ; and poor Jessie, shrinking from her, went to her uncle, laid her head upon his shoulder, and wept.

"The shoe has begun to find holes in the stocking," said Uncle Morris, passing his hand over Jessie's head, with great tenderness ; " but never mind, my little puss—cheer up. Your cousins will leave their bad tempers in the land of dreams, I hope, and their good-nature will return with the sun to-morrow morning. Dry your eyes, my sweet Jessie, and be thankful to the Father above, that your cousins cânnot rob you of your own sunny temper."

Jessie did dry her eyes, and looking into her uncle's face, said, with a nod of her pretty head, "Now I know why you sighed ; and I know, too, what your proverb meant."

" What did I sigh for, puss ?"

" Because you knew my cousins had ugly tempers."

"That's so !  But the proverb ?"

" Meant that when I became better acquainted with my cousins, I should find out their faults."

"Well done, my little puzzle-cracker. You are good at guessing. But, Jessie, what are you going to do? How will you treat your cousins to-morrow?"

Jessie held down her head awhile, as if she was thinking her way through a difficult idea. At last she looked up, with eyes full of tenderness, and with a voice made musical by deep feeling, said:—

"I will be just as kind to them as I possibly can!"

"That's right, my Jessie," said her uncle, folding her to his bosom and kissing her forehead, "that's right. There is nothing like kindness for curing ugly children. It's the best medicine in the world to give them. Give it to them, Jessie, in big doses. Maybe they will like it so well that they will get cured of their ugliness; for, as the proverb says,— *Flies are caught with syrup; not with vinegar.*"

"Wouldn't it be nice, Uncle Morris, if we could make my cousins good-natured while they are here? Wouldn't Uncle Albert and

Aunt Hannah be glad if we could send them
home kind, and gentle, and good? Oh, I wish
I could get them to be good, as our Guy did
Richard Duncan. Wouldn't it be nice?"

"Try to do it, my dear. We will all help
you, and so will the Great Father above," said
Mrs. Carlton, beckoning Jessie to her side and
giving her a kiss so full of a mother's holy love
that it sent a thrill of bliss through the happy
heart of her child. Thus like a sunbeam did
Jessie brighten the life of her parents and her
uncle. As she left the room to go to bed,
Uncle Morris followed her with his eyes, and
when her light form had glided up-stairs, he
turned to his sister and said:—

"That child of yours is a treasure, my sister.
I can't tell you how much her loving little
heart gladdens mine. Why, I have grown at
least fifteen years younger in my feelings since
she came to Glen Morris. Like a glorious
little sun, she shines into the depths of my
heart, melting all the ice of age and chasing
away the gloom of my past sorrows."

"Yes, Jessie is a lovely child," replied Mrs.

Carlton. A big tear which dropped upon her needle-work at that moment showed that the words of her brother had stirred the deep foun tains of love which were within her heart.

But the two ugly cousins—what were they ? Were they not like two black clouds freighted with storms, and come to darken the light and disturb the pleasure of that happy household ? No wonder their sleep was troubled that night. No wonder Emily awoke in a fright, caused by the terrible nightmare. But Jessie's sleep was sweet and sound, and when her mother stood over her bed, as she always did before retiring for the night, Jessie smiled so sweetly in her slumber that her mother said :—

"Bless her! the smile of a seraph is on her lips."

As Uncle Morris foretold, Emily and Charlie left their sulks in dreamland. It would have been well if they had left the *selfishness*, from which their conduct of the evening before sprung, in the same place. But that still clung to them like the leprosy, and though they wore bright faces, they still carried fireworks in their bosom, ready to explode whenever a spark might happen to touch them.

Jessie greeted her cousins with gentle words and loving kisses, just as if she had never seen them in a fit of bad temper. Indeed, she made no allusion whatever to the affair of the day before. This silence puzzled the cousins, who expected, at least, a lecture from Uncle Morris and a little coldness from Jessie. I think it also made them feel ashamed, for they could not help saying to themselves,—

"It was rather mean in us to make such a fuss as we did yesterday."

Just after breakfast, while Jessie was showing Emily her six dolls, neither of which had a perfect dress, for Jessie never *finished* any thing, and Charlie was playing with Guy's india-rubber ball in the hall, Hugh plunged in at the front door, and, rushing into the sitting-room, said :—

"Jessie, what will you give me if I tell you a secret?"

"A kiss," replied Jessie, gathering her lips into the form of a rose-bud.

"Pooh! what's a kiss. I wouldn't give you a red cent for a thousand kisses. Won't you offer me something better for my secret?" said Hugh, turning up his nose as if in scorn of the proffered kiss.

"I don't believe you have any secret that we care about knowing," said Jessie. Then holding up her best wax doll, she said to Emily, "Isn't this a beauty?"

"Yes, but why don't you coax Hugh to tell us his wonderful secret?" said Emily, who felt quite curious to know what Hugh had to tell.

"Oh, he is only teasing us. You don't know what a tease he is," replied Jessie, with an air of indifference.

"No, honor bright, I'm not teasing. I have a secret that would make you girls pitch your dolls into next week, if you knew it," retorted Hugh.

"Well, what is it? Do tell us," said Jessie, beginning to believe that he had something to tell worth knowing.

"What will you give me?" asked Hugh, still bent on tantalizing the girls.

"I've got nothing to give that you want," said Jessie, and then in a coaxing tone she added, "come, Hugh, do tell us, there's a good, dear Hugh."

"No, you don't come it over me with soft soap like that," replied the boy; "I'm not a fly to be caught with maple molasses."

"If you was *my* brother I'd *make* you tell me," said Emily, her eyes sparkling with rising passion as she spoke.

"You *are* a spunky little lady, I declare," said Hugh, laughing; "but here, Jessie, suppose you try to *guess* my secret. It is something you would give ever so much to know."

"*Really*, Hugh, have you a secret, *truly?*"

"Yes, *truly*. Honor bright, I tell you. It is a glorious secret. It will make you ever so happy to know it."

"What is it about? Is somebody coming here? Do tell me, Hugh."

"Catch a weasel asleep and you'll catch me answering questions. But I see you *won't* buy, and you *can't* guess my secret, so I'll be off," and in spite of all the entreaties of Jessie and the biting speeches which Emily made, master Hugh left the room, carrying his secret with him.

Jessie, sighed, and turning to her dolls, said, "Hugh is a great tease, isn't he Emily?"

"He's a great ugly monster!" retorted Emily, who was in the habit of using strong words, without much regard to their meaning. "If he was my brother he shouldn't tease me so."

"Oh, Hugh only does it for fun. He is a dear good brother, after all, only," and here Jessie lowered her voice almost to a whisper, "only I wish he was as good as Guy."

"*For fun*, eh? I'd *fun* him. I'd pull his hair, and hide away his books, and steal his playthings, and call that fun, if he was my brother," cried Emily.

"Oh, fy! cousin Emily. That would be wicked fun, and would make both you and your brother unhappy," said Guy, who had just entered the room.

The girls looked on the speaker, who, before Emily had time to reply, went on to say,—

"Girls, Carrie Sherwood invites you to go

nutting with her this afternoon. Richard Dun
can, Norman Butler, Adolphus Harding, Wal·
ter Hugh, Charlie, you two young ladies, Car·
iie, and a young lady or two of her acquaintance,
are t' make up the party. Carriages will call
for you at one o'clock. You must get ma to
give you an early dinner, and be ready in time."

"That is what Hugh meant by his secret.
Oh, I'm so glad," said Jessie, clapping her
hands. "Won't it be nice, Emily?"

Emily thought it would. The girls thanked
Guy for his good news, and, springing from the
sofa, started to inform Charlie and Mrs. Carlton
of the proposed party. Charlie was delighted.
Mrs. Carlton knew all about it, because the
whole matter had been quietly arranged a day
or two before by her and Mrs. Sherwood. Car·
ried away by the idea of this delightful ex·
cursion, Jessie left her six dolls, with their
incompleted dresses, on the sofa, on the chairs,
and on the floor. IMPULSE, the merry little
wizard, had seized her, and she thought of
nothing but the nutting-party the remainder
of the morning.

# CHAPTER III.

## A NUTTING-PARTY.

A FEW minutes before one o'clock, a long, spring market-wagon, drawn by two noble horses, stopped before the gate of Glen Morris Cottage. It contained Carrie Sherwood and her party, all but the Carltons and their visitors. Mr. Sherwood sat on the driver's seat. He went with the young folks to drive, and, as he quaintly said, "to see that the hawks did not pounce on his chickens;" by which figure of speech, I suppose, he meant that he went to keep the young folks out of danger.

Jessie and her guests, together with Hugh and Guy, were all waiting when the carriage drove up. Shouts of welcome greeted them from the wagon. They gave back cheer for cheer as they sprang to their places, all but Charlie, who stood near the front wheel pout ing, and looking very sulky. Mr. Sherwood, who had turned half round to watch the seating of his guests, did not notice the boy, but supposing the party to be now complete, faced his team, drew the reins tight, flourished his whip and shouted—

"All aboard!"

"Charlie is not aboard yet," cried Emily.

"Come, Charlie! Jump up here!" shouted half a dozen voices.

"I don't want to," said Charlie, in a drawling tone.

"Don't you wish to go, my little fellow?" asked Mr. Sherwood.

"I want to sit on the coachman's seat," simpered the boy, as he stuffed his finger into his mouth.

The driver's seat was not meant for two persons, and Mr. Sherwood was in doubt whether to crowd Charlie into it or not. But seeing from the boy's manner that he would spoil the pleasure of the party if he did not, and being a very indulgent man, he at last consented. So pulling him up to the footboard, he stowed him away by his side, and cracking his long whip, drove off amidst a volley of cheers from the boys, the laughter of the girls, and the waving of handkerchiefs by Mrs. Carlton and Uncle Morris, from the piazza.

"I want to drive!" muttered Charlie, as soon as they were fairly started.

"You must eat a little more beefsteak, and grow a little taller, my boy, before you undertake to drive such a span as this," replied Mr. Sherwood, smiling at the boy's presumption.

"I *will* drive!" growled Charlie, grasping the reins, and giving them a jerk, which startled the spirited creatures into an uneasy gallop.

"Whoa there, steady Kate, steady!" said Mr. Sherwood, removing the boy's hands and reining up his team.

After soothing his horses, and bringing them to a gentle trot again, Mr. Sherwood took his reins in his right hand, and, grasping Charlie with his left, suddenly jerked him over the driver's seat, into the bed of the wagon, saying,

"Boys! take care of this little coachman!"

This was not so easily done. Charlie's ugly temper was up. He tried to scramble back to Mr. Sherwood's side, but the larger boys held him firmly in spite of kicks and blows which he dispensed without ceremony, until, fairly tired out, he sat down on the floor of the wagon, biting his thumbs and looking like a lump of ill-nature. This display of ugliness spoiled the pleasure of the drive. It was worse than a shower of rain, for it threw a black cloud over the spirits of the party, and made them all unhappy.

They had not fully recovered their cheerfulness, when they came to Duncan's pond, and in sight of old Joe Bunker's flagstaff, from the top of which the stars and stripes proudly floated in the fine breeze of that October afternoon.

"There's the bunting you gave old Mr. Bunker!" observed Guy to his friend Richard.

"Yes, there it is, sure enough, and old Timbertoe is as proud of it as a little boy is of his first pair of pantaloons," said Richard, laughing at the oddity of his own comparison.

"Or, as Richard Duncan was, of that famous

shot from his pea-shooter, which hit Professor Nailer's long nose," said Norman Butler, chuckling and rubbing his hands, at the recollection of that exciting scene at the Academy, a few months before.

"Or, as my sister Jessie is of her Uncle Morris," said Guy.

Mr. Sherwood's loud whoa! whoa! and the stopping of the horses in front of Joe Bunker's barn, put an end to this series of comparisons. This was the place where they were to leave the horses; for butternut-trees were quite numerous in some extensive pastures which were situated round the shores of Duncan's pond. "Old Joe" welcomed the party, and put up the horses, while the boys pulled out the baskets from beneath the wagon-seats, and made ready for the nutting.

But Master Charlie was not yet rid of his sulks, and would not stir from the wagon. He wanted to go home, he said; he didn't care for nuts, and would not go with his companions. In vain did his sister entreat, Mr. Sherwood command, and Jessie try her coaxing powers

LITTLE WILL, the celebrated child conqueror, was playing the tyrant over him; and the unhappy boy gave himself up, hand and foot, to his enemy. He would not quit the wagon.

"Never mind! leave him where he is, until his good-nature comes back, if he has any," said Mr. Sherwood.

"I am afraid he will get into mischief after we are gone, if we do that," said Guy. "Perhaps I had better stay here and mind him."

"You shall do no such thing with my consent, Guy. Go with the rest, and I'll put this cross urchin in charge of Mr. Bunker," replied Mr. Sherwood. Then turning to the old sailor, he added;

"Look here, Mr. Bunker! We have a little bear in our wagon, that don't seem to like nuts. Will you keep your eye on him while we go into the pastures?"

"Ay, ay, Sir," said Old Joe, giving his waistband a hitch. "I'll keep a bright lookout for him."

Leaving Charlie under the old sailor's care, the party now set out in search of nuts.

Laughter and pleasant words beguiled both
time and distance, and for the next two hours
they wandered over the pastures, and picked
up an abundance of butternuts, which several
pretty hard frosts, followed by strong breezes,
had scattered plentifully on the ground, or prepared to fall quite readily from the trees.

In the course of the afternoon, the party
separated into little groups, and when it was
nearly time to return to the wagon, it happened
that Jessie and her cousin, lured by the sight of
a large butternut-tree in the distance, found
themselves apart from all the rest. Near the
tree was an old stone-quarry, with numerous
lakelets in the hollows from which the stone
had been removed. Emily stepped into the
quarry, and looked all around. The lakelets,
swept by the light breeze, charmed her eye,
and turning to her cousin, she cried:

"Jessie, come here! Here are some tiny
ponds. Come look at them!"

Jessie joined Emily, and together the little
girls stepped over the uneven rocks until they
reached one of the lakelets. There they launch-

ed small pieces of wood, called them ships, and
stood watching their mimic fleet in great glee.

After spending some time in this way, they
heard the voice of Guy calling :

"Halloo! Halloo! Jessie! Emily! Halloo! Halloo!"

"We must go," said Jessie, "I guess they
are going back to the wagon."

"No, don't go," replied Emily. "Let us
frighten them a little—just a little, by making
them think we are lost."

"Wouldn't it be funny!" said Jessie, clapping her hands, and feeling charmed with the
idea of getting up an excitement among her
companions. IMPULSE, the little wizard, had
followed her, even into that old quarry !

"It will be first-rate fun," said Emily.
"How they will search for us! It will be as
good as a game of hide and seek."

"Halloo! Halloo! Jessie! Emily! It's
time to go home! Halloo-o!" shouted Guy
again from the pasture. The wind being fair,
his words were heard quite distinctly by the
two girls.

JESSIE AND EMILY SAILING BOATS IN THE QUARRY.    Page 51.

"There is a little cave just big enough to hide in," said Emily pointing to an excavation in the highest wall of the quarry. "Let us go into it!"

Still yielding to the voice of the little wizard, and thinking only of the excitement which was to follow the supposition she was lost, Jessie followed her cousin into what she called "a cave." There was water at the bottom, but a flat piece of rock rising above the water enabled them to get to the back part of their "cave," where they were pretty well concealed from view.

Again the voice of Guy shouted Jessie's name. This was now followed by a chorus of voices, all calling—

"Halloo!—halloo!—halloo-oo-oo!"

The voices drew nearer and nearer, until the callers stood on the edge of the quarry.

"Where *can* they be! I'm afraid they are lost! Oh, dear, what will mother say, if we have to go home without them!" said Guy, distinctly enough for Jessie to hear.

"Perhaps they have fallen into some old well," suggested Norman.

"I think not," said Mr. Sherwood. "I doubt if there is an old well in all these pastures. They have most likely wandered back towards the pond."

"I don't see how that can be," rejoined Guy, "for I saw them running in this direct... half an hour ago. Besides, we found their basket under that tree, and they would not have gone to the pond without telling some of us to bring their basket."

"There's no telling what silly things girls will do. I guess they are gone to the pond. Suppose we go and see."

This was Hugh's voice, and as no one proposed any thing else, the party left the quarry, and, hallooing as they went, directed their steps towards the pond.

"Let us run after them!" said Jessie, who now began to feel as if she had carried the joke far enough.

"Hush! you little coward," said Emily, placing her hand over Jessie's mouth. "They aren't half frightened enough about us yet."

Jessie tried to get her mouth away from her

cousin's hand. In doing so she stepped backwards, and, losing her balance, fell with a splash into the water.

"Oh!" cried she, in a great fright. But the water was not deep, and the side of the "cave" kept her from falling entirely down. Hence, a thorough fright and wet feet and dress were the only evil results of her misstep.

"Pooh! what a silly little goose you are," said Emily, in a taunting tone of voice. "If you had done as I told you, you wouldn't have got that wetting."

"I'm afraid I have done too much as you told me already," replied Jessie, crying, "and now I'm going right after our party, as fast as I can."

With these words Jessie stepped out of the cave, tripped across the quarry, and ran out into the open pasture; Emily, not liking to play "lost child" all alone, followed her. But their party was no longer either in sight or within hearing, for an elevation in the ground rose between them and the two girls.

"Guy! Hugh! Richard! here we are!" screamed Jessie, at the top of her voice.

Vainly did she scream, however. The wind blew the sounds back upon herself, and she began to run in the direction of the pond.

"Don't be in such a hurry," said Emily, hanging back.

"We *must* hurry," replied Jessie, "or we shall be really lost. See, it's almost sundown! And it is so damp and chilly that I am shivering with cold. Come, Emily, do make haste, there's a dear, good cousin."

"If I am your *dear, good cousin*, you won't drive off and leave me," retorted Emily, still lingering and moving only at a snail's pace.

"Oh dear! what shall I do!" exclaimed Jessie, looking very wretched, and she certainly felt as unhappy as she looked.

"Wait for me!" said Emily, "that's what you *ought* to do!"

Thus urging her stubborn cousin, Jessie pressed forward as fast as she could get her companion along.

Meanwhile the rest of the party had hastened towards Joe Bunker's stand. On their arrival they found the old sailor at tea in his little cottage. Rushing somewhat wildly into the room, Guy said,—

"Mr. Bunker, have you seen my sister since we left?"

"Your sister, skipper?" said the old salt "Shiver my topsails if I've seen any thing in the shape of a gal, except this old craft of mine here, since you all left your wagon early this afternoon."

"Then she and her cousin are *lost*," said Guy, driving his hands deep down into his pockets, casting his eyes to the ground, knitting his brows, and walking out into the open air again.

"Are they there?" "Has the old cove seen them?" "What does old Timbertoe say?" with half a dozen other questions, greeted Guy as he crossed the threshold.

"Hasn't seen their shadow. They must be lost," replied Guy, doggedly.

"Is that spunky little Canada thistle you call Charlie in the house?" inquired Mr. Sherwood.

"I didn't see him. Isn't he in the wagon?"

"No sign of him that I can see," replied Mr.

Sherwood; "but here's Mr. Bunker—Mr. Bunker, where is the little boy we left in your care?"

"I left him making sand-cakes down on the beach a few minutes ago," said old Joe.

All eyes were now turned to the beach, but no Charlie was to be seen. Old Joe looked uneasy as his eye swept the shore. Very soon he gave his waistband an unusual hitch, brought down his wooden leg with great force, and said:—

"As sure as my name's Joe Bunker, the little fellow is gone on a cruise in the Little Susan!"

"Gone on a cruise? What, alone?" asked Mr. Sherwood, looking a little pale.

"Yes, alone, or I'm no sailor."

Down to the shore of the pond they hurried. Sure enough, the Little Susan was gone. Charlie, in opposition to Mr. Bunker's command, had gone aboard and, sitting amidships, had rocked her to and fro until her painter had got loose, and the wind, which blew off shore, had drifted the boat out on to the pond, where she was now visible, with Charlie's head just above the bulwarks, steadily setting down towards a a point about a mile distant.

"To the Point! Make for 'Long Point!'" shouted old Joe.

Away ran the boys, with old Joe hobbling after them, Guy only remaining behind with the girls and Mr. Sherwood. Charlie's danger had for the moment driven all thought of Jessie and Emily from their minds. Now, however, they began to consider what was to be done to recover the lost cousins.

"I see them!" shouted Guy, pointing to the hill-top in the distance, and starting to meet them. They were just visible in the distance. He soon reached them, very much to Jessie's relief. Tenderly kissing her he said—

"Where have you been, Jessie?"

"We missed our way, and got lost in the woods behind that horrid quarry!" said Emily. "It's a wonder we ever found the way back again."

"Oh, fy—" cried Jessie. She would have said more, and have contradicted this wretched lie, but Emily put her hand before her mouth while she poured a long story of pretended adventures into Guy's ears. Jessie was shocked. She thought of her uncle's sigh, and of his quaint proverb, and was silent.

It was fairly dark when the Little Susan, steered by Joe Bunker, with Charlie and the other boys on board, touched her dock. The horses being by this time harnessed to the wagon, the party with their freight of nuts, were soon rolling homewards. Very little was said, after Emily, interrupted by frequent "ohs!" from Jessie, had repeated her lie about losing their way. All felt that the pleasure of the occasion had been greatly marred by Charlie's conduct; and in spite of Emily's lie and Jessie's silence, they also felt that if Jessie should speak she would make it appear that Emily's story was not exactly true. But the reader *knows* that all the shadows which fell upon that excursion came from the selfishness of the two visitors from Morristown.

# CHAPTER IV.

AT the tea-table Emily told a long story about herself and Jessie wandering away into the woods, and getting sadly frightened. She was very animated, and, but for Jessie's sad face, and her occasional look of surprise, might have made herself believed. But that grave face, so unusual to his darling Jessie, told Uncle Morris that Emily was palming off a falsehood upon them. Guy also was sure she was telling a lie. When she had finished her story, he said,

" But did you not hear us shout and halloo ?"

" No, indeed. If we had, we could have easily answered back," said the lying child.

" O Emily !" groaned Jessie.

" We shouted like one o'clock !" said Hugh.

" Pray tell us, Master Hugh, what shouting like one o'clock means ?" asked Uncle Morris, who had a very great dislike to unmeaning phrases.

"Well, very loud, then," replied Hugh, blushing.

"But you didn't shout loud enough for us to hear," said Emily, secretly pinching Jessie, by way of imposing silence upon her.

"It's very strange," said Guy. "It was certainly not more than ten minutes from the time we left the quarry, before we saw you coming over the top of the hill in the pasture, so that you could not have been very far in the woods when we were shouting like—like—"

"Like boys in search of two young ladies supposed to be lost or *hidden*," said Uncle Morris, helping Guy to a comparison, and at the same time hinting his suspicions of the truth in the case.

Jessie blushed deeply and was about to speak, when Emily, growing fiery red with anger, said:

"Well, if you don't choose to believe me, you needn't, but I don't think it's very polite to talk to me as if you thought I was telling you a lie."

Seeing that her young guest was fast losing her temper, and that Master Charlie was nodding over his empty plate and tea-cup, Mrs. Carlton rose from the tea-table, and addressing the two girls, said :

"Perhaps, as you are wearied with your excursion, my dears, you had better retire now, and finish your talk about it to-morrow, when you are rested.   Come, Charlie, open your eyes and go to bed !"

"Let me alone !" growled the drowsy boy, as his aunt took his hand to lift him from his chair, and lead him from the room.

Jessie sighed, and looked as if she too had a story to tell when she kissed her Uncle Morris good-night.  The old gentleman returned her kiss very affectionately, and whispered,

"Jessie, you make me think of the proverb which says, *The day that the little chicken is pleased, is the very day that the hawk takes hold of him.*   Good night, dear !"

Jessie was puzzled, and all the way up-stairs kept saying to herself, "What can Uncle Morris mean? what can Uncle Morris mean?"

And while undressing she said still to herself, "I can't be the chicken, because I'm not pleased—but stop—Yes, I was pleased this morning. Perhaps, then, I'm the chicken. And the hawk—must—be—well—it must be Emily! Ah! I see now. He thinks Emily has made me do some wrong to-day. And he is right too. It was wrong to hide away in the quarry. It was worse to pretend not to hear when the boys called us. That was *acting* a lie. And it was wrong for me to keep still when Emily made up that wicked story about our getting lost. Oh dear! Oh dear! How sorry I am! I wish I hadn't hid away in the quarry!"

"What makes you look so glum, Miss Solemn Face?" asked Emily, who, without kneeling down to say her evening prayer, was getting ready for bed as fast as her nimble fingers could move.

"I am thinking that I did wrong to-day, replied Jessie, sighing deeply and standing motionless in the middle of the chamber.

"Fig's end! I never knew such a girl as you

are. *Wrong* indeed! Just as if it was wrong to have a little fun," replied Emily, sneering.

"Fun is not wrong; but it was wrong to alarm Mr. Sherwood and the boys, about our safety. I know they felt very bad when they thought we were lost. It was wrong, too, for us to pretend not to hear when they called us. That was *acting a lie*. And oh, Emily! how *could* you make up that wicked story, about our getting lost in the woods!"

Jessie spoke with such deep and solemn feeling, that Emily's conscience was touched. A slight shudder passed over her as she buried her head in the pillow, and drew the bed-cover close to her face. Her voice was a little husky, too, when she replied:

"You are too fussy, by half, Jessie. Good-night!"

"Good-night!" said Jessie; and then dropping to her knees, beside the big arm-chair, the well-taught child began to think over the events of the afternoon. The longer she thought, the more guilty she felt. She could not say her prayers, because her sin rose before her mind

like a great, black cloud.  At last, she began to
weep and sob, saying in half-audible whispers:

' I'm so sorry!  I'm so sorry!  I wish I
hadn't made believe I didn't hear!  Oh dear!
oh dear! what shall I do ?"

Emily got up a mock snore, by way of saying, "I'm asleep, and don't know but that you
are asleep too."  But she was not asleep, nor
did she feel like sleeping in the least.  In fact,
she kept peeping over her pillow at Jessie, and
wondering why she felt so bad, until a voice
within her, whispered:

"If Jessie feels bad for yielding to your
wishes, how ought *you* to feel, who led her
astray, and who told such a shocking lie to
hide your fault?  Emily Morris!  Emily Morris!  You are a wicked girl!"

Jessie now rose from her knees, bathed in
tears.  Wrapping herself in a dressing-gown,
she took the lamp in her hand, left the room,
and went, with slow and heavy steps, down
stairs.  Leaving her lamp on the hall-table, she
went into the parlor.  Every eye was lifted
towards her, with inquiring glances.  She went

directly to that sweetest of all earthly nestling-places for a child in sorrow, her mother's arms, and whispered:

"O mother! I've been a naughty girl to day!"

Mrs. Carlton drew her closer to her heart, kissed her with great tenderness, and said:

"What has my child done?"

Jessie wept violently, and was silent, for her heart was too full of emotion, to coin its thoughts into words. Mrs. Carlton, like a sensible mother, said nothing until the floods of Jessie's grief passed away. Then smoothing her head with her hand, she spoke in tones, so soft and lute-like, that they sounded like sweet music in Jessie's ears, and said:

"Tell me, my dear, what troubles you so much?"

Thus soothed, Jessie raised her head, and said:

"I want Pa and Uncle Morris to hear, too."

Mr. Carlton laid aside his book. smiled, and said:

"I'm all attention, Jessie."

5

Uncle Morris drew his chair close to Jessie, patted her head, and said:

"That's right, my little puss, make a clean breast of it. Confession is the pipe through which the great Father conducts the guilt of his little ones, when, for his Son's sake, he buries it in the fountain of forgetfulness."

Thus encouraged, Jessie gave a full account of how she came to hide in the little cave with Emily. When she had finished her story, Uncle Morris said—

"Ah, I see, the little wizard has been busy again. I'm sure it was he who helped Emily to tempt my little puss. An *impulse* acted upon you, Jessie, and, without thinking, you hid in the cave, which was not a very grave fault in itself; but, as most little faults will do, it led you to commit a really serious evil; as you say, by pretending not to hear yourself called, you *acted a lie*, which was a sin against God. You also filled your party with alarm about you, which gave them great pain of mind. That was an offence against them, because it was your duty to do all in your power to afford them pleasure. The hawk did, indeed, catch my chicken on the day that she was pleased. Do you understand my proverb, now, Jessie?"

"Yes, Uncle, but what shall I do?"

"Do, my child? There is only one way by which any of us can escape from the chains of evil. Confess your *sin* to God, ask his forgiveness for the Great Shepherd's sake, and appologize to your friends for giving them pain."

Jessie said she would do both of these things. Then her heart turned to her cousin, and she said—

"But what shall I say to Emily?"

"Just tell her your own thoughts and feelings about the matter, my child. Maybe, she will be led to see the wrong of her own conduct, and you may yet be to her what your brother Guy has been to Richard Duncan."

After making this remark Uncle Morris took the old Family Bible and read a psalm of penitence. Then he and the family kneeled down to pray. The dear old man seemed to speak

right to the Good Father in behalf of his sorrowful little niece. And while he pleaded the love
of the great Shepherd for his precious lambs,
Jessie felt as if a heavy burden rolled away
from her heart, the big black cloud passed from
before her eyes, and the sweet springs of joy
and gladness once more poured their streams
over her happy spirit.

With a light step, Jessie tripped back to her
chamber. Emily was still awake. Thoughts
such as she had never cherished before were
rushing through her brain and burning in her
heart. She was strongly inclined to speak to
Jessie. But pride set a seal upon her lips, and
she kept her eyes closed in simulated sleep.
As for Jessie, after whispering a prayer for
Emily and a song of praise for herself, she laid
down beside her cousin and slept as sweetly as
a fairy in a blue-bell, or as a weary angel might
slumber in one of the bright bowers of Para-
dise. You may be sure her dreamland was
filled with images of love and beauty.

The next morning Jessie awoke wondering
how Emily would feel about the events of the

day before. Finding her cousin was also awake, she said—

"Emily!"

"Good morning, Jessie," replied Emily, sit ting up in the bed and looking full in Jessie's face. "I hope you feel more cheery than you did last night."

"I am very happy this morning,"· replied Jessie, her eyes sparkling with delight as she spoke. "Shall I tell you how I came to be so?"

"As you please!" said Emily, shrinking from Jessie's proposal as if she feared her story might bring back the guilty feeling of the night previous.

Jessie told her cousin just what she had felt, and how she had confessed her wrong, and how her sorrow had been rolled away. She did this so simply, so sweetly, and so kindly, that Emily blushed, and the big tears stood like dew-drops on her eyelashes. Jessie had found the way to her cousin's heart.

But when she urged her to confess her faults and to join her in a note of apology to the Sher·

woods, the pride of Emily's heart rose within
her, and dashing away her tears, she said—

"*Apologize*, indeed!   I won't do it!"

Just then the ringing of the first breakfast-bell
warned them that it was time to rise.   They
did so; and Jessie, seeing that her cousin did not
wish to talk any more, dressed herself in silence.

After breakfast Jessie went to her writing-
desk, and wrote notes to the members of the
nutting-party.   These notes were all alike except in their different addresses.   Here is a
copy of the one for Mr. Sherman.

GLEN· MORRIS COTTAGE, October 25, 18—
DEAR SIR—

When you thought I was lost
yesterday, I was hiding with my cousin in a
little cave in the stone quarry.   I only did is
for fun.   If I had thought my hiding there
would make you feel bad and spoil the pleasure
of our nutting-party, I would not have done it.
I am sorry I did it.   Will you, and Walter, and
Carrie, please excuse my fault?

Truly Yours,
JESSIE CARLTON.

MR. WALTER SHERWOOD, SEN.

When Jessie read one of her notes to Uncle Morris, the good old man patted her head, and said—

"Nobly and sweetly written, my little puss Never forget that next to avoiding a fault, the noblest and most honorable thing you can do, is to confess it and apologize for it. Still, I hope you may never have need to write such a note again."

Having finished and sealed her notes, Jessie placed them carefully in the bottom of her work-basket, intending to ask Hugh to deliver them for her on his way to school in the afternoon.

It was Mrs. Carlton's wish that during her cousin's visit, her daughter should spend part of every morning, sewing and reading. Hence, after the notes were nicely put away, Jessie took out her famous piece of patchwork, and began sewing. She laughed heartily as she did so this morning, because she found pieces of paper pinned to the articles intended for Uncle Morris with these words written on them in large letters—

"Beware of the devices of the little wiz-ard!"

"Ha! Ha! Ha!" laughed she. "Won't I beware? I'll sew, let me see; well, I'll sew a strip long enough to go once around my quilt before I stir, let the little wizard say what he will."

Stitch, stitch, stitch, went Jessie's bright, swift, little needle for the next half-hour. Then her two cousins bounced into the room, shout-ing—

"O Jessie, come and see! There is one of the funniest little men out here you ever did see. He's got no neck, and he wears the queerest sort of a hat! He's playing on the bagpipe. Come, just a minute."

"Beware of the devices of the little wiz-ard!" said the writing on the patchwork. It caught Jessie's eye just as she was going to drop her work and run out to see the funny little man. She felt as if something was twinging her heart, but remembering her purpose, she brought her work to her side, and said—

"I thank you, cousins, but you must excuse me until I've finished my sewing."

"What a cross thing she is!" said Charlie, bouncing out of the room.

"Do come, just for a minute, that's all, cousin Jessie," said Emily in her most coaxing tones.

Charlie's words wounded Jessie more than Emily's soothed her. Unwilling to be thought cross, she dropped her work "just for a minute," and went out. The queer little man excited her mirth greatly, and she soon forgot all about her patchwork. When the little pipe-player moved off, Emily said—

"Let us follow him up to Carrie Sherwood's. Won't she be tickled to see him?"

"Yes, do," said Charlie, "and I won't call you cross, Jessie, any more."

"We mustn't stay long, then," replied Jessie reluctantly, for a thought of her sewing flashed across her brain.

"Of course, we won't," said Emily, as she took her cousin by the hand and led her away. "We will only stay long enough to see Carrie laugh at the queer little man."

They went to Carrie Sherwood's, and there they stayed until Walter's return from school warned Jessie that it was nearly dinner-time. As she re-entered the parlor she saw Uncle Morris point to her work lying as she left it on the floor, and heard him say—

"The little wizard has been here again, I see, this morning. How fond he is of Glen Morris Cottage."

Jessie blushed, ran to her Uncle's side, hid her face in his bosom, and whispered—

"O Uncle, I never shall conquer that little wizard. He is too strong for me."

"Never despair! my little puss. Try and try again. Make a new resolve, and I'll warrant you that the wizard will find Glen Morris Cottage too hot to hold him one of these days, and then he'll be off to the North Pole to keep cool, and perhaps to marry Miss Persever-ance!"

Jessie laughed at this conceit of her uncle's, and said—

"Uncle, I will try again, and I'll try real hard next time."

"Nobly spoken, my little lady," rejoined Mr. Morris. "Perseverance conquers all things. It has won victories for warriors; freedom for oppressed nations; and self-conquest for millions of men, women, and children. Hold on to your purpose then, my Jessie, and you will yet be crowned as the conqueror of your troublesome little enemy !"

Jessie sighed, and looked as if she wished the last battle had been fought, and the crown already placed on her brow.

Poor Jessie ! she is not the first miss who has found it hard work to overcome Little Impulse, the wizard.

# CHAPTER V.

When Jessie saw Hugh getting ready to go to school, after dinner, she thought of her notes which were still lying very snugly in her work-basket. There were four of them: one for Mr. Sherwood, one for Richard Duncan, one for Adolphus Harding, and one for Norman Butler. Taking them from beneath her working materials, she held them up, and turning to Hugh, who was on his way to the door, said—

"Hugh, I want you to do me a little favor!"

"I dare say. You girls are always asking favors. But what now?"

"Not much, Hugh, I only want you to take these notes for me."

"Notes, eh?" said Hugh, taking the neatly folded letters in his hand, and reading the ad dresses. After reading them all aloud, he placed them in a pack and added. "Pretty business, I think, for a young lady like you to be writing to the boys? Oh, for shame, Jessie Carlton! I thought you were too modest to do that!"

"There's nothing improper in my notes, master Hugh! Uncle Morris read one of them, and he says they are very sweet and proper. Will you please take them for me?"

"Yes, if you will pay me the postage on them. You know that Uncle Sam gets his pay beforehand, and I must have mine. So hand me over twelve cents, and I'll carry your notes. Come, be quick! Hand over your money! It is time I was gone."

"O Hugh, don't tease so," said Jessie.

"Do you call it *teasing* to ask for your pay when you are going to work for anybody!" asked Hugh, with a very tantalizing air.

Just then Guy passed through the parlor, and seeing that Jessie was getting tired with her vexatious brother, he asked what was the matter. She told him. He took the notes from Hugh, who was only too glad to give them up, and said—

"I'll take them for you, Jessie."

"You are a dear, good brother, and I love you ever so much," said Jessie, holding up her lips for a kiss.

Guy kissed his sister and hurried away to school, happy in the thought that he was contributing to her pleasure, while Hugh went out with a cold, uneasy heart, and murmuring to himself—

"I don't see why I should wait all the time on Miss Jessie; she's big enough to carry her own letters."

Could Hugh have exchanged feelings with Guy, he would have learned that little acts of love and kindness bring rich returns into the hearts of those who perform them; and then, perhaps, he would have seen at least one reason why he should "wait all the time on Miss Jessie."

It happened that afternoon to blow up cold and rainy, so that Jessie and her young guests could not play out of doors. The bright fire in the grate tempted them into the parlor, where they amused themselves in various ways. At last wearied with quiet games, master Charlie said—

"Let us play blind-man's-buff?"

"Oh yes, do, Jessie! It's such good fun," said Emily.

"I like it first rate," said Jessie. "Who will be blind-man first?"

"I will," said Emily, in a very positive tone of voice.

"No, you won't, either, I shall be blind-man first," said Charlie.

"Well, I say you *shan't*. There now!" cried Emily, stamping the floor with her little foot.

"But I tell you I *will!*" retorted Charlie with anger.

"Hush! Charlie dear," said Jessie, in sooth-ing tones. "Let Emily be blind-man first, for, you know, polite boys always give way to young ladies."

"Well, I won't, I don't want to be polite, I want to be blind-man first, and I WILL," re-joined Charlie, as the fire flashed from his eyes.

"Then I won't play at all," said Emily, going to an ottoman and seating herself in a very sulky mood.

Thus did these unamiable cousins spoil their own p'easure, and give pain to Jessie by their selfish quarrel. In vain did she try to soothe and coax them into good-nature for some time. At last, tired of the attempt, she rose up, and said—

"Well, if you won't play, I'll go into the library and have a good talk with my Uncle Morris."

This movement made Emily feel slightly ashamed of herself. She was unwilling, too, to be left alone with her brother. So she jumped up, and with a forced smile, said—

"Don't go, Jessie, I'll let Charlie be blind-man."

"I've a great mind not to play with you at all now," growled Charlie.

"Oh yes, do, there's a dear, good Charlie," said Jessie, as she approached him, "See! here is the handkerchief, let me tie it over your eyes so that you won't be able to see the least bit of a mite! I don't think you will be able to catch me before tea-time."

This challenge did more to drive the sulks out of Charlie than the coaxing. Charles held his head forward to be bound, while he replied—

"Can't I catch you! I'll bet a dollar I catch you in less than five minutes!"

"Young ladies *don't bet*, and Uncle Morris says that boys *shouldn't*, because it's wicked,'' said Jessie, while she busied herself tying the handkerchief. When the knot was fast, she said—

"Now let us see how skilful my cousin Charlie can be!"

Up jumped Charlie, spreading out his arms, and darting now this way and then that, as the steps and voices of the girls led him round the room. Merrily rang out the laugh of Jessie, and the ohs and ahs of her cousin, as they bounded past Charlie, run round him, or darted out of the reach of his nimble fingers. So spry were they, that ten minutes elapsed and the blinded boy had not caught either of them. At last, he followed them close to one end of

6 ·

the parlor until he found himself clasping the
large mirror which reached almost to the floor.
Stepping back he tripped over a low ottoman,
fell backwards, and bumped his head.  Half i..
vexation, and half in sport he threw up his
heels, and just as Jessie cried, "Mind the glass,
Charlie!" brought down his legs with a crash
on the surface of the mirror.

"Oh dear!  He has broken the big mirror!"
cried Jessie, in great distress.  "What will my
father say!"

"Keep still, you stupid, mischievous boy!"
said Emily as she tried to pull the bandage
from Charlie's eyes.

"I couldn't help it!" said he, as rising to his
feet, and rubbing his eyes, he stood staring on
the ruin his feet had wrought on the lower half
of the mirror.

"My pa paid a good deal of money for that
mirror," said Jessie, "and he will be very
angry with us, when he comes home to-night.
I'm *so* sorry."

"That's just like you, you stupid little
monkey," said Emily, shaking Charlie some-

what rudely by the shoulder. "You are always doing some outrageous thing or another!"

"I couldn't help it! Let me alone!" muttered Charlie, shaking his sister's hand from his shoulder.

"You *could* help it," replied Emily.

"There, take that!" said Charlie, striking his sister a heavy blow on the shoulder with his fist.

Emily was about to strike back, but Jessie stepped between them, and separating them, said:

"O Emily! don't strike your brother! It's *so* wicked, you know, for brothers and sisters to fight." Then turning to Charlie, she added, "Don't you know how mean it is for a boy to strike a girl? Boys should protect girls, and not beat them. If you hit Emily again, I shall not be able to love you any more."

Charlie turned away, and seating himself in a chair, began to suck his thumb, while he gazed on the broken glass which was spread over the carpet. Just then, old Rover, finding

the parlor door ajar, pushed it open, and walked up to his young mistress, wagging his tail,
and rubbing her hand with his nose, which was
his way of saying, "I hope you are glad to see
me, this afternoon."

Jessie patted his head, and sat down wear-
ing a very grave face. Rover thought something was amiss, but not knowing how to
inquire into the matter, after a few more rubs
of his nose upon his little lady's hand, laid
down, and looked wistfully into her eyes.

Rover's presence put a new idea into the evil
mind of Emily. She turned it over silently a
few moments, and then said:

"Jessie! I have just thought of a capital
way of getting out of this scrape about the
mirror."

"Have you?" replied her cousin. "I don't
see how you can do that, unless you can get
some fairy to mend it for us, and I guess there
are no good fairies, to do such things for
unlucky girls and boys, now-a-days."

"*Fairies* indeed!" retorted Emily with a
sneer. "I don't believe in *fairies.* My plan is

to tell your mother, that while Rover was playing with us, he bounced against the mirror,
and broke it to smash."

" O Emily! I would not tell such a wicked
story to save my life?" rejoined Jessie.

"Well, I would; I've got out of many a bad
scrape, by fixing up some such story as that.
And it is so *natural*, you see, for a big dog to
bounce against a glass which is so near the floor
as this one, that your folks will easily believe
it."

"O Emily! Emily! How can you talk so?"
said Jessie, gazing at her cousin with an expression of pity and surprise.

"She talks just right," said Charlie. "It's a
first-rate story, and will get us out of the scrape
nicely. Bravo, Emily! I won't hit you again
for ever so long."

Jessie was horror-struck to hear her cousins
talk in this cool and hardened manner. To her
mind a lie was of all things the most mean and
wicked. She had just shown her hatred of it,
by her penitence for merely acting a lie in fun
But this proposal to tell a downright lie, for the

purpose of escaping the consequences of an
unlucky accident, looked like asking her to
commit a very shocking crime. She felt a
shudder creep over her, and shrinking from her
cousins, as if they had been deadly serpents,
she pushed her chair back a yard or two, and
said:

"Emily, I would die before I would tell such
a lie. I hope you won't think of doing it. It's
*so* wicked, Emily. If you could deceive my pa
and ma, you couldn't deceive God, who saw
Charlie break the mirror. Don't do it, Emily,
please don't?"

"We will do it too, and if you peach on us,
we'll say it was your fault that Rover did it.
How will you like that, Miss Jessie!" said
Charlie.

"I will tell my father the exact truth about
it," said Jessie, rising to her feet.

"Very well, Miss Tell Tale," retorted Emily.
"We'll fix you then. Charlie and I will say
that you threw the ottoman against the mirror,
and broke it yourself, won't we, Charlie?"

"Yes, and they will believe both of us,

because they will think you are lying to escape
being whipped for your fault. Ah! ah! Miss
Jessie, we'll fix you, see if we don't!" and
Charlie held up his finger, and grinned in his
cousin's face.

"My father knows I wouldn't tell a lie,"
replied Jessie firmly; "and I do hope you
won't, for oh! it is *so* wicked, and *so* mean.
Nobody loves, trusts, or believes a liar. Please
Charlie, please Emily, let me tell pa just how it
happened. He won't be very angry. I know
he won't. But if he is, I will tell him to whip
me, instead of scolding Charlie."

Charlie winced under this noble speech of
Jessie's, and for a moment was inclined to
yield. But his sister's temper was roused, and
she urged him to stick to her, and to say that
Jessie threw the ottoman, "and now," said she,
"I will go and tell my aunt directly."

Jessie turned pale; not with fear for herself,
but because she shrank from a conflict with her
cousins, in her mother's presence. Fortunately, a happy thought came into her mind, and
rising, she whispered to herself, "Yes, I will go

and ask Uncle Morris to come in." And Jes sie glided into the library.

Her uncle was not there. He had left 't an hour before, and feeling slightly dozy had gone into the back parlor to catch a little nap on the sofa. This parlor was separated from the one in which the children had been playing only by folding-doors. Their noise at blind-man's-buff, had roused him from his nap, and he had heard all that afterwards passed between them. When, therefore, Emily went to tell Mrs. Carlton her great lie, he thought it was time for him to interfere. So he passed round by the hall into the front parlor, just as Jessie with her sad face was returning from the library.

"Oh, I'm so glad you are here, Uncle Morris!" exclaimed Jessie, her face brightening and growing much shorter. "Please come into the parlor."

The good old man kissed his niece with even unusual tenderness, and led her into the parlor.

"Hoity toity!" cried he, as he looked on the fragments of the broken mirror. "Somebody's been playing the mischief here. What's been the matter?"

"Jessie did it!" said Charlie, with a dogged air.

"Yes, sir! Jessie threw an ottoman at me, and it struck the mirror. Didn't she, Charlie?" said Emily, coming up to Uncle Morris, with Mrs. Carlton behind her.

"Yes, Jessie did it, and no mistake!" said Charlie, boldly.

"O Jessie! how could you be so careless! That mirror cost a hundred dollars, a few months ago. Your father will feel very an- gry," said Mrs. Carlton with a grieved look.

"I did not break it, Ma!" said Jessie calmly.

"She did!" "She did!" said Charlie and his sister in the same moment.

"Ma, I did not break the mirror," rejoined Jessie, calmly. "If I had done it, I would confess it. You know I wouldn't lie, Mother, don't you?"

"I certainly have great faith in your truth- fulness, my child," replied Mrs. Carlton; "but why are your cousins so positive in charging you with it?"

Jessie stated the facts just as they had taken place. Her cousins repeated their story. Mrs. Carlton was perplexed. Turning to Uncle Morris, she said :

"Brother, what do you think? On which si le is the truth ?"

"On Jessie's, of course, sister. Could you question the truth of that pure face! It would break my heart if Jessie could tell such a lie as these wicked ones here have told! But she couldn't do it. It's not in her nature to do it. Heaven bless her!"

He then stated what he had overheard from the sofa in the back parlor, and closed by saying, "These children had better go home to-morrow. They are wicked enough to corrupt an angel, almost. The proverb says, *eggs ought not to dance with stones*, and I cannot endure to see Jessie in their society any longer."

"I agree with you, brother, and will send them home to-morrow," replied Mrs. Carlton.

Charlie and Emily were dumb with confusion and shame. I think a little sorrow gushed up in Emily's heart, when through her fingers she saw Jessie look with appealing and tearful eyes into Uncle Morris's face, and heard her say in pleading tones:

"O Uncle! O Mamma! please let them stay another week; please do, for my sake! Please let them stay! They will be good after this, I know they will."

This plea won both Mrs. Carlton's and the old man's consent, and Jessie kissing her cousins, said:

"There, you can stay. Aren't you glad?"

# CHAPTER VI.

### THE FIRST SLIDE OF THE SEASON.

AFTER Uncle Morris and Mrs. Carlton had consented to permit the self-willed cousins to remain a week longer at Glen Morris, the good old man led Emily into the library and talked with her for over half an hour, about the meanness and wickedness of lying. I cannot tell you exactly what he said to her, because I don't know. That his words were weighty and solemn, I have no doubt; for when Emily left the library her eyes were red with weeping, and she went directly to her room and staid there alone until the bell called her to tea.

Before Emily slept that night, she did what she had not done before during her stay at Glen Morris. She kneeled at the bedside to say her prayers. When she arose, Jessie threw an arm around her waist and kissed her. This was done with so much tenderness, that Emily felt it to be a sign of her cousin's sympathy with the new feelings and thoughts which were springing up within her heart. Returning the kiss, she said :

" I'm sorry I told that lie about you to-day Jessie."

" So am I," replied the simple-hearted girl; " it is always best to tell the truth, and I hope you will never tell another story as long as you live."

" I won't, I'm resolved I won't; I told Uncle Morris so this afternoon, and (here she lowered her voice to a whisper) I've been asking God to help me keep my promise."

" That's the way ! That's the way !" replied Jessie. " Uncle Morris says if we mean to be good we must go to school to the Great Teacher who will both teach us, and help us do the lesson."

With such words as these did Jessie encourage her cousin to enter that beautiful path in which all the pure, noble, and good children in the world are found.

The next day Emily was very quiet. She
spent the morning helping Jessie work on her
famous quilt. Charlie was as rude and as ugly
as ever; having teased his sister for a long time
in vain, to play out of doors with him, the
spoiled boy hissed at her, and said, "You are
an ugly old cat!" Then slamming the door
after him, he went into the barn-yard, where
the screaming of the pigs, the gabble of the
geese, and the clucking of the hens, soon pro-
claimed that he was venting his ill-temper on
the dumb creatures who had their home there.
Poor Charlie! the indulgence of his mother,
and the almost constant absence of his father
from home, had made him a very unhappy,
mischievous boy, if, indeed, it had not wholly
spoiled him. If Charlie had known what was
best for him he would have said to his friends,

"Please don't let me have my own way."

Emily needed to make the same request, for
she too, had long done pretty much as she
pleased; and, as we have seen, she was *pleased*
to do some very bad things.

Two days before the time set for the cousins

to return home, they went to spend the day with Carrie Sherwood. Jessie, who was to join them after her morning's sewing was done, sat down to her work in high spirits. The quilt had grown large within a few days, and as she took it up this morning, she said :

"The little Wizard hasn't been able to catch me for ever so many days. I guess he won't trouble me much more now. See my quilt! (here she stood up, and drawing the quilt from the basket, spread it out.) Two more rows of patchwork will finish it. Ha! ha! only two more ; I'm so glad. And won't Uncle Morris be pleased when he sees it spread over his bed some night! ha! ha!"

Here Jessie sat down and began to make her bright little needle fly almost as swiftly as if it had been in a sewing-machine. While she sewed she hummed the following words, which, as Uncle Morris said, had more truth in them than poetry :

"I love to do right,
    And I love the truth,
    And I'll always love them,
    While in my youth.

"And when I grow old,
  And when I grow gray,
I will love them still,
  Do wrong who may."

Having finished her song, Jessie rested her hands on her lap a moment, and said: "I love those words, I do. When I grow *gray!* ha! ha! Jessie Carlton a little old woman with *gray hair!* Won't it be funny? I wonder if everybody will love me then as everybody loves Uncle Morris now. Why not? Everybody?—no, not *everybody*, for Charlie don't love him, and our Hugh don't love him much. That's because they are naughty, though. Well, every good person loves Uncle Morris, because he is so good and kind; and so, if I am good and kind, when I am a little, gray old woman, everybody will love me. Ha! ha! Won't it be nice to be called Aunt Jessie, and to be loved, oh, so well!—but I must go on with my sewing."

Tap, tap, tap, said somebody's knuckles on the door.

"Come in," cried Jessie.

The door opened. Carrie Sherwood's little, red, round, laughing face peeped in.

"O Carrie! is that you? Come in."

Carrie tripped in, and while her eyes flashed with excitement, she said :

"O Jessie, we have found a nice slide out on the edge of the brook. It is the first time the ice has frozen hard enough to bear this fall, and we are having such a nice time. Come and see it, just for a moment."

"A slide!" exclaimed Jessie, who dearly loved sliding. "Oh, I'm so glad. I'll go with you just to look at it. I can't stay, you know, because I must come back and sew until twelve o'clock."

Dropping her sewing, Jessie ran to a closet, equipped herself in cloak and hood and, taking Carrie's hand, trotted out to see this first slide of the season.

A short distance from Glen Morris Cottage a broad, shallow brook crossed the public highway. A bridge led over the brook. Along the sides of the buttresses of this bridge, the water had flowed back for several yards over the bottom of a ditch or hollow, and being only an

7

inch or two in depth, the sharp frosts of the early days of November had frozen it solid, though the brook itself was still babbling as if in proud defiance of the frost-king.

To this ditch Carrie led Jessie. Emily and Charlie were already there enjoying themselves finely.

"Isn't it nice?" said Carrie when they had fairly reached the spot.

"You shan't come on to my slide," growled selfish Charlie.

"Nor on to mine," cried his sister.

"You will let us slide after you, won't you, Emily?" asked Jessie.

"No, I want this slide all to myself," replied Emily.

"You can go down the brook and find slides for yourselves. You shan't use ours," cried Charlie, as shaking his fist at the two girls, he added, "I'll lick you both if you don't keep off."

"Well, I never saw any thing so selfish as that before, I declare," said Carrie Sherwood, striking the ground with her foot, and looking very angry as she spoke. "The next time I in vite them to spend the day at my house they shall certainly know it."

"Oh, never mind, never mind," said Jessie. "We can look at them, and that will be almost as good as sliding ourselves. Perhaps they will get tired presently, and then we can slide while they rest."

"No, we shan't get tired either, Miss Jessie," retorted Charlie. "We mean to slide until dinner-time."

"And then you expect to eat dinner at *my* house, I suppose. Really, you are a very generous boy !" replied Carrie, in a bitter tone of voice.

"'Taint *your* house. It's your father's. He !" said the ugly boy, grinning at his young hostess.

"Well, if you were not Jessie's cousins, you should never step inside of my house again— but here comes my brother. He'll *make* you let me slide."

Walter Sherwood now came up to the spot where his sister and Jessie stood. Carrie told him the story of the selfishness of the two cousins, and ended by saying :

"Won't you compel them to let us slide too, Walter?"

"If he touches me, I'll throw this big stone at him," growled Charlie, looking very ugly and holding up a large stone, which he had just taken up from the side of the ditch. Wasn't he a selfish little fellow?

"Please don't touch him," entreated Jessie "I don't care much about sliding, and Carrie won't mind waiting until to-morrow. Will you, Carrie dear. The weather is so cold, there will soon be plenty of ice. Please don't hurt Charlie, Walter."

"Don't be alarmed, my sweet Jessie," replied Walter, laughing. "I don't want to touch your sting-nettle of a cousin. I'd about as lief grapple a hedgehog. Let him and his selfish sister have their slides all to themselves. You come with me. I know where there is far better sliding than this, and I came on purpose to tell you so. Come, let us go, and leave them to enjoy their slides, if such selfish creatures can enjoy any thing."

"Please Walter, let my cousins go with us,"

whispered Jessie in Walter's ear, as he took her hand.

"No, no, Jessie, I can't consent to that. They won't be a whit happier there than here, and if we do take them with us, they will only spoil our fun. I never saw two such thorns in my life. You can't go near them, but they scratch you right off."

"They are going home, the day after to-morrow, and I'm glad of it," cried Carrie, as she stepped up the bank after her brother and Jessie.

"So am I," said Walter, "and I'm thinking there will be plenty of dry eyes at Glen Morris Cottage, when they go away. What do you say to that, Jessie?"

"I'm sorry my cousins are so selfish," replied Jessie, "but Charlie is the worst. I think if Emily was here without him, she would soon be a good girl."

"Perhaps so. Yet I'm inclined to think you'll see apples growing on that old hickory yonder, before she becomes *good*, as you call it. But let us hurry into the pasture. Here, Jessie, mount these bars?"

As he spoke, Walter leaped over the rail-fence of a pasture, and giving his hand to Jessie, she mounted the top bar.

' Now jump!" cried Walter.

Jessie did as she was told. Carrie followed. Then Walter led them along the pasture, until they struck a bend in the brook where the water having flowed over a flat basin, was very shallow. Along the edge of this basin the water was frozen hard.

"Isn't this nice?" shouted Jessie, as she slid over the glass-like surface.

"It's perfectly beautiful," replied Carrie, gliding along in an opposite direction.

Walter made a slide for himself, just in front of the girls, and being all brim-full of good-nature, they enjoyed themselves finely. But there were two shadows that flashed on Jessie's joy now and then. The first was the image of the quilt she had left on the parlor-floor ; the second was her regret that her cousins were so ugly. When the former image flitted before her, a little voice in her breast whispered,

" In the chains of the little wizard again, eh ?"

JESSIE AND CARRIE ENJOYING A SLIDE.          Page 105.

Then Jessie would sigh, look very sober, and pause, saying to herself, "I really must go home and sew."

Before her purpose was fairly formed, how-ever, Walter or Carrie would cry out, "What, getting tired already! You are not half a slider."

"Just once more, and then I'll go," Jessie would say to herself. But before that one more slide was through, she would purpose to add yet another. Thus time fled until the morning was almost gone, and the quilt, the little wizard, Uncle Morris, and even the ugly cousins, were nearly forgotten, in the excitement of this pleasant sport.

This delight was, however, brought to an end by a loud scream, followed by a shrill voice crying, "Charlie! *Charlie!* CHARLIE! You'll be drowned? Oh dear! Oh dear!"

This was followed by another scream. Wal-ter guessed what was the matter at once. He knew that near where the cousins were sliding, the trunk of a tree formed a sort of bridge over the brook, and enabled the cow-boys to pass dry-shod in summer. When the brook was low, it was a safe enough bridge, but when it was full as it was then, it was what the boys called "a pokerish place to cross." He surmised at once, that Charlie was frightening his sister, by attempting to walk across the brook on this rough and narrow bridge. So he told the girls, and then they all ran towards the spot from whence the cry came.

A few minutes' run brought them in sight of Master Charlie standing erect on the tree, right over the middle of the brook. Emily was standing at the water's edge, screaming, and begging him to come back.

"Stop your screaming, you coward, or I'll lick you till you are dumb," shouted the wilful boy, shaking his fist at his sister, as Walter and the two girls came up, on the other side of the brook.

Emily seeing them approach, called out to Walter, and said:

"Do make him come off that dreadful log, will you?"

"I'd like to see anybody *make* me come off,"

said Charlie. As he spoke, he turned round to see who had come. In doing this his foot slipped, and losing his balance, he fell backwards into the brook.

The girls both screamed, for they were in great terror. Walter, however, laughed heartily, and said :

"Don't be frightened! The water isn't deep enough to drown the little fury. I hope it's cold enough to cool his courage, though."

As he spoke, Walter rolled up his pants, and then kicking off his boots, he waded into the brook and led Charlie ashore. The little fellow spluttered and shivered, but said nothing. The water had cooled his courage, and for the present, his ugliness had all subsided. They led him back to Glen Morris as quickly as possible, to get a change of clothes.

This mishap broke up their plan of dining and spending the afternoon with Carrie Sherwood. Thus the selfishness of the two cousins, again robbed both themselves and their friends of a promised pleasure. As for poor little Jessie, she drew down her face and looked very

sad, as she put her quilt into the basket, when
the bell rung for dinner. Sighing deeply she
said half-aloud,

"Conquered again. It *is* no use. The little
wizard *is* my master, and I won't try to resist
him any more. What's the use of trying?"

"Tut, tut, tut! No use in trying, eh? Who
says so?"

Jessie looked up, and her eyes met the pleas
ant smile of Uncle Morris, who had entered the
room, in his usual quiet way, unobserved by
the dispirited girl. She gave him back no
answering smile, but drooping her head, stood
silently before him. Seeing her sadness and
knowing the cause, Uncle Morris said:

"Jessie, will you please be a school-ma'am
for a moment, and let me recite my lesson to
you?"

Jessie smiled a faint smile, but said nothing.

"Well, silence gives consent, I suppose. So
I will recite my lesson. It is a fable and runs
thus:

"Two robin redbreasts built their nests
Within a hollow tree;

The hen sat quietly at home,
    The male sang merrily ;
And all the little robins said,
    ' Wee, wee, wee, wee, wee, wee.'

One day—the sun was warm and bright,
    And shining in the sky—
Cock Robin said, ' My little dears,
    'Tis time you learn to fly ;'
And all the little young ones said,
    ' I'll try, I'll try, I'll try.'

' I know a child, and who she is
    I'll tell you by and by,
When mamma says, ' Do this' or 'that,'
    She says, ' What for ?' and ' Why ?'
She'd be a better child by far,
    If she would say, ' I'LL TRY.' ''

When Uncle Morris paused, tears stood in Jessie's eyes, and a bright smile played round her lips. Putting her hand into his, she said:

"And I'll try, too, Uncle. I'll try till I con-quer."

# CHAPTER VII

AFTER dinner Jessie went to her room and sat awhile, on a cricket with her head leaning on a chair. She was thinking. I cannot tell you exactly what passed in her mind, while she was in that brown study, because she never told me. You can guess, however, when I tell you that after thinking some five minutes, she rose up, and going to her table, took a pencil and wrote these words in big letters, on a sheet of note paper:

"I will not go out to play again until I have finished my quilt. This is my strong resolution, and I mean to keep it, in spite of the little wizard that tempts me so. He has beaten me a great many times, but he shan't do it again, as true as my name is Jessie Carlton."

Taking the paper from the table, Jessie held

it between her finger and thumb, read it, and
then left the room, saying to herself—

"There, that's a good resolution. I'll keep it
in sight all the time; and if the little wizard
comes near me, I'll spear him with it just as
Uncle Morris says the fairies pierce the gnats
with their bodkins. Let me see. How long
will it take to finish my quilt. Only two more
rows of squares to sew on. Well, I can sew
one row this afternoon and the other to-morrow
morning. Oh good! I'll ask ma to get it into
the quilting-frame to-morrow afternoon, and
have it finished while I work the slippers.
Won't it be nice if the quilt and slippers are
both ready by Christmas! Perhaps I can get
the watch-pocket done too. Well, I'll try, see
if I don't. I *can* conquer little Impulse if I try,
and I *will*. You shall see if I don't, you dear,
good Uncle Morris, you."

All this was said as Jessie walked down-stairs.
She looked very pleasantly, and trod the carpet
with a very firm step, as she went to her cosy
little chair in front of the bright fire which
glowed in the grate that November afternoon

She was slightly chilled through sitting in her chamber, but without stopping to get warm, she took up her work, and began to ply her needle in good earnest.

Half an hour passed and Jessie was still busy as a bee over her quilt. Then her uncle entered the room with his outside coat nicely buttoned up to his chin, and his hat in his hand. He was equipped for a walk.

"Jessie, will you take a walk with your poor old uncle this fine afternoon?" said he.

This was offering one of the strongest of possible temptations to Jessie. A walk with Uncle Morris was to her a very great pleasure. Impulse whispered "Let the quilt go, and accept your uncle's offer!" Jessie's arms were even put forth in the act of dropping her work, when her eye rested on her written resolution, which she had pinned on the top edge of the work-basket. "I will finish my quilt," said she down in her heart. Then putting her work back into her lap, and looking up at her uncle, who was a little puzzled by her unusual manner, she said—

"I thank you, Uncle, but I can't go this af-ternoon."

"Not go! What does my little puss mean?" exclaimed Uncle Morris, greatly surprised that his niece should decline his invitation.

Jessie took the paper from the basket, gave it to him, and, while a loving smile played round her lips, said—

"Please, Uncle, read this."

The old gentleman put on his spectacles. glanced at the paper, and, as he gave it back to her, smiled, and said—

"Ha, ha, I see! going to run the little wizard through the heart with the spear of Resolution! Very good. I would rather see you conquer your enemy, my dear Jessie, than to have your company, much as I love it. So good-by, and may the Great Teacher help you to keep your resolution!"

"Good-by, Uncle!"

I can't tell you how happy Jessie felt at hav-ing resisted this strong temptation. A warm current of joy flowed through her heart, and bore away all regret which thinking on the loss of a pleasant walk might have otherwise caused her to feel. Her eyes sparkled with delight. Her fingers almost flew, and the quilt gained in size very fast.

But fifteen minutes more had not passed, when Emily and Charlie bounced into the room.

" We want you to play with us," said Emily. "We are tired of playing together without company, and want you."

" I want you to play horses I've got some twine for a pair of reins, and you two girls will make a capital span. Come, hurry up, Jessie!" said Charlie, who had got over his ducking in the brook, and was as rude and ready for mischief as ever.

" I'm very sorry," replied Jessie, " but I can't go with you. I must sew on my quilt till tea-time."

"*Must*, eh! Who says you *must ?*" replied Emily with a sneer.

" I have made a resolution to punish myself for going out this morning when I ought to have stayed in," said Jessie, firmly.

" Pooh," said Charlie, " that's all nonsense.

She is too proud to play with us. She is a regular Miss Stuckup, and I won't own her for my cousin any more;" and with this hard speech the boy left the parlor, walking backwards, and making mouths as he went.

"I do think you ought to play with us, Jessie," said Emily. "You know we have only one day more to spend with you, and it's very unkind of you to stay in here and leave me to amuse myself as best I can. As to your resolu tion, I s'pose you made it on purpose, because you didn't want to play with us."

This unkind speech made Jessie feel very badly. She doubted for a moment whether she had not erred in making her resolution before her cousins went home. She felt inclined to drop her work, and go out with her very ungracious cousins. But her second thoughts assured her that it was her first *duty* to conquer the habit which had caused her so much trouble. So looking with moistening eyes at her cousin, she replied—

"I'm sorry, Emily, that I cannot go out with you, but I really can't do it. You know my

8

ma requires me to spend my mornings in sew
ing or reading. I went out this morning with
out thinking, and without asking her consent
To make up for that, I must sew this afternoon
This evening and to-morrow afternoon, I will
play with you as much as you please."

"I say you are a very ugly creature, and I
don't like you one bit," retorted Emily, as with
pouting lips and flashing eyes she bounced from
the room, slamming the door with a loud noise
as she went out.

Poor Jessie felt wounded, and the big tears
would flow from her eyes in spite of her efforts
to restrain them. Smarting under the cruel
words of her cousin, she felt an impulse to fol
low her, but again her eyes fell on the paper,
and she resumed her work, saying to herself—

"Jessie Carlton, you must not mind the hard
speeches of your cousins. Your resolution is
right and good. Uncle Morris said so. Stick
to it then, and by the time the quilt and a few
other things are done, as Uncle Morris said, the
little wizard will find Glen Morris Cottage too
hot to hold him. I'll keep my resolution."

Just then, smash went some glass somewhere in the rear of the house. The crash was fol lowed by a voice, which Jessie knew to be her cousin's, saying—

"O Charlie, Charlie! what have you done!'

"I don't care! It's only the kitchen win dow," was the reply.

Again did Jessie's impulse move her to put down her work and run out to see what was the matter. But her purpose came to her aid again, and she kept plying her needle and saying:

"No, I won't go out. It's only that naughty Charlie throwing stones in at the kitchen window. What a bad boy he is. I'm glad he is going home soon."

Another quarter of an hour passed without interruption, when the door opened and the bright face of Carrie Sherwood peeped in.

"Why, Carrie Sherwood!" exclaimed Jessie.

"Jessie Carlton!"

"Come in and sit down," said Jessie.

Carrie stepped in but did not sit down "I've come," she said, "to invite you and your cousins to spend the afternoon, and to take tea at our house. Ma says that since no harm came to Charlie from his ducking, she would like to have you come as you meant to do before he fell into the brook."

"I can't go with you till nearly tea-time," replied Jessie.

" Why not?"

" Because I *can't.*"

" But *why* can't you?"

" Because I've resolved to sew on this quilt until tea-time," said Jessie; and pointing to the paper she added, "see! there is my resolution."

Carrie read the paper and laughed. "Well, you are a queer girl, Jessie Carlton. You tie yourself up with a resolution nobody asks you to make, and then say you can't move."

"But I made the resolution because I thought it was *right,*" said Jessie, solemnly.

"Oh! did you? Well, that alters the case, I suppose. But please break it for *once; only* this once, just to please me, you know. Come, there's a dear, good Jessie; do come over to my house this afternoon."

Oh! how Jessie did long to drop her sewing, and go with her friend. There was a mighty struggle in her heart for a few moments; but her purpose triumphed at last, and in a calm, firm voice, she replied :

"No, dear Carrie, not until nearly dark. I must finish my quilt to-morrow morning. You go and get my cousins and take them with you. I will come over just as soon as it is too dark to see to sew without a light; and that won't be a great while, you know, this short afternoon."

Carrie saw that her friend's mind was made up. So turning to leave the room she said :

"Well, I suppose you are right; but mind you come as early as you can."

"That I will," rejoined Jessie.

Carrie left the room. The next moment she pushed the door open again, and peeping in, said,

"Jessie ?"

"Well, dear, what is it ?"

"Ask your ma to let you stay till half-past nine, will you ?"

"Yes."

"Good-by."

"Good-by till dark," replied Jessie, laugh
ing at the idea of her friend bidding her good
by just for an hour.

Jessie now felt very strong in her purpose
She had resisted no less than four temptations
to yield to her impulses in about an hour and a
half. This was doing nobly, and Jessie felt
more self-respect than she had ever felt before.
She was certainly doing battle in real earnest
with her old enemy, the little wizard, as Uncle
Morris facetiously called him. And she had
her reward for all her self-denial in the glad
feelings which bubbled up in her heart like
springs of water in some cosy mountain nook.

Nothing else came to tempt Jessie the remainder of that afternoon. She sewed until it
was too dark to see in front of the fire; then
she took her seat close to the window, and it
was not until she could no longer see to take a
stitch neatly that she began to put up her work.

"One more morning will finish it," said she,
after taking a glance at her work. "Oh! how
glad I shall be when I have taken the last

stitch.   And won't I be glad when it comes out
of the quilting-frame, and is spread upon Uncle
Morris's bed.   It's been a long time doing—
Oh! ever so long—thanks to the little wizard.
But little wizard, little wizard, go away! go
away!   We don't want you any longer in Glen
Morris Cottage."

In this cheerful mood Jessie tied on her hood
and cloak, and tripped over to Carrie Sherwood's, where she spent one of the pleasantest
evenings she had enjoyed since the coming of
her cousins to Duncanville.   For some reasons
unknown to me, it pleased that selfish brother
and sister to put on their best and most approved behavior.   Perhaps they caught a ray
or two of the joy which beamed, like sunshine,
from Jessie's heart.

The next morning after breakfast, filled with
the idea of finishing the quilt before dinner,
Jessie found a parcel in her work-basket directed to Miss Jessie Carlton.

"What can it be?" said she, as she hastily
untied the string, and unfolded the wrapping
paper.

"A pair of ladies' skates! Oh, how glad I am! I wonder who sent them. Oh! here is a piece of paper. What does it say?"

Holding the paper to the light she read as follows:

"From a fond father to his beloved daugn ter."

"From pa! Oh, how good of him! It's too bad he didn't stop to let me thank him. But I'll thank him to-night. I've been wishing all this fall for a pair of skates, because all the girls are going to have them. Suppose I just step out and try them a little while."

Thus did Jessie talk out her thoughts to herself. Thus did the impulse come over her to leave her morning's duty and repeat the fault of the day before. It was fortunate, perhaps, that her cousins, knowing she meant to sew, had rushed off to find a slide before she discovered her new skates. Their persuasions joined to her own impulse, might have over come her and brought her into bondage to the little wizard again. Without their presence, I confess, the temptation to try the skates was a very strong one. Jessie was getting ready to go out when her eye fell on the paper which was stil' pinned to the basket's edge. She paused, blushed, put down the skates, and said aloud :

"No, no, little wizard, I won't obey you. The quilt shall be finished, and the skates shall wait until the afternoon."

"Three cheers for my little conqueror!" shouted Uncle Morris, who, coming in at that moment, overheard this last remark.

" O uncle! I was *almost* conquered myself," said Jessie.

" Never mind that, for now you are *quite* a conqueror," rejoined her uncle, smiling and patting her head.

Need I say that the quilt was finished that morning? It was; and before Jessie sat down to dinner, she had the pleasure of seeing it put into the quilting-frame by Maria, the seamstress of the household. And thus did our sweet little Jessie win her first really decisive victory over the little wizard which had hitherto been to her like the fisherman's wife, Alice, in the fairy tale—the plague of her life.

# CHAPTER VIII.

SCARCELY had Jessie feasted her eyes on her quilt, snugly fixed between the bars of the quilting-frame, before the dinner-bell rang out its pleasant call. The happy girl skipped downstairs with a light and merry step. In the hall she met her brothers.

"O Guy!" she exclaimed, "I have finished my quilt! Aren't you glad!"

"To be sure I am," said Guy, kissing her rosy cheek, "and I expect you will be so well-pleased with my old friend, Never-give-up, who helped you finish it, that you will never give him the mitten again."

"Pshaw!" cried Hugh with a sneer, "I'll bet my new knife, that she gives him the mitten before the week is out. Jessie isn't made of the right stuff for your famous Try Company,

any more than I am. She hasn't got the perseverance of a kitten."

"And yet she has more of it, than Master
Hugh Carlton, for he has never finished any
thing but his dinner, and she has finished her
*quilt*," said Uncle Morris, who as he was cross-
ing the hall to the dining-room, heard Hugh's
unkind remark.

"There, Hugh, you are fairly hit now," said
Guy, laughing.

"They who live in glass-houses shouldn't throw
stones, should they, my little puss?" said Uncle
Morris, leading Jessie into the dining-room.

"Hugh is always teasing me," replied Jessie,
"I wish he was more like Guy."

Dinner was waiting, and taking their seats at
the table, they all sat in silence, while Uncle
Morris reverently craved a blessing. He had
hardly finished, before Charlie and Emily
rushed into the room, leaving traces of their
feet on the carpet, at every step.

"My dears, where have you been to wet
your feet so?" asked Mrs. Carlton, seeing that
their boots were soaked with water

"Oh! it's been thawing, Aunt, and we got our feet wet, sliding," said Emily, as she took her seat at the table, panting and pushing the ringlets back from her face.

"You had better put on dry socks and boots, before you eat," observed Mrs. Carlton. She then touched the bell. The servant entered.

"Mary," said the lady, "take these children to their rooms, and change their socks and boots!"

"Yes mem," said Mary, looking daggers at the two cousins.

"Can't I wait till after dinner, aunt?" asked Emily.

"No, my dear. You must go at once, lest you get cold by sitting still so long with wet feet."

Emily pouted, but knowing her aunt would firmly enforce her command, she rose, and taking her brother by the wrist, said:

"Come, Charlie, let us go up-stairs!"

"I don't want to," growled Charlie, pulling away his arm, and putting it round his plate.

"Charlie!" exclaimed Mrs. Carlton.

"I want my dinner!" was his surly reply.

Mary had now drawn near the ugly little fellow. Placing her heavy hand on his shoulder, she seized him with a grip, which made him feel like a pigmy, in the grasp of a giant. Having had a taste of Mary's anger, once or twice before, and catching a glance from the kindling eye of Uncle Morris, he yielded, and was led out of the room.

"The worst child of his age I ever knew," observed the old gentleman with a sigh, as he proceeded to carve the chickens, which were smoking on the hospitable table before him.

Jessie's face had clouded a little during this scene. The thaw of which Emily had spoken, cut off her hope of trying her new skates. Leaning towards Guy, who sat next to her at the table, she whispered:

"Is the ice *all* gone, Guy?"

"I expect it is pretty much used up by the fog we've had all day."

"Oh dear, I'm so sorry!" said Jessie with a sigh.

Judging of her thoughts by her looks, Uncle

Morris said, "Never mind, Jessie. There will be plenty of ice to skate on, in a week or two,"

"Skate! How can she *skate?* She hasn't got any skates!" said Hugh.

"Yes, I have," replied Jessie smiling. "Pa sent me a beautiful pair this morning."

This statement led to various remarks about skating, and winter weather in the country. Meanwhile, the cousins came back to the table. Jessie soon grew cheerful again, and the dinner passed without any other occurrence worthy of notice.

After dinner, the fog having grown into a fine, drizzling rain, the children found it impossible to go out of doors in search of amusement. It was therefore agreed to invite Miss Carrie Sherwood to tea. Guy promised to go after her. To add to the pleasure of the occasion, Jessie had her mother's permission to use a sweet little tea-set of her own, and to have tea with her cousins and Carrie by themselves in the parlor.

Carrie arrived in due time, snugly wrapped in hood and shawl. Her feet were protected by rubbers. She declared that Guy was a capital *beau.* Guy laughed at her compliment, and re-paid it by saying that she was a nice little *belle,* and then he ran off to school.

The afternoon passed rapidly, because, on the whole, it was pleasantly spent. Emily, know-ing it was the last day of her visit, seemed anxious to do away with the bad impression she had previously made upon the mind of her cousin and her friend. Charlie, too, was in his best mood most of the time. Once, indeed, he came very near breaking up the harmony of the party. Seeing a strap of Jessie's new skates peeping from beneath the what-not where she had hidden them, he seized it, pulled out the skates, and began to put them on.

" Please, Charlie, don't do that," said Jessie, " You can't skate on the carpet, you know ; please give them to me ?"

" I won't !" retorted the wilful boy.

" Please do give them to me ?" implored Jessie.

" I want to skate on the carpet, first," said Charlie, still trying to buckle on the skates.

"Do ask him to give them to me?" said Jessie, addressing Emily.

"There, take your old skates!" cried the boy, throwing them violently across the room.

The fact was, he did not understand the mystery of straps and buckles in which the skates were involved. Hence his desire to try the skates was borne away upon the current of his impatience, and thereby the little party escaped a scene for the time being.

But it was only for a time. Charlie had been so used to have his own way and to oppose the wishes of others, that he seemed to find his pleasure in spoiling the delights of others. Hence, when the hour for tea arrived, and Jessie's sweet little china tea-set, with its ornaments of gold and flowers, was spread out upon a little round table, he drew near to it and taking Jessie's seat, said:

"I'm going to play lady and pour out the tea."

"Nonsense, Charlie!" said his sister. "Take the next seat and let Jessie have hers."

"I won't," muttered Charlie.

"Come, Charlie, do get out of your cousin's

chair! Young gentlemen don't pour out tea for ladies, you know," said Carrie in her most coaxing tones.

"I don't care! I'm going to play lady and pour out the tea," replied the boy in his most dogged manner.

"I never did see such a boy in all my life," whispered Jessie to her friend.

"Nor I," rejoined Carrie; "my father says he's a young hornet."

"Oh dear! what shall I do?" sighed Jessie.

"Why don't you sit down?" said Charlie, as he began to handle the little teapot.

"Charlie, get up!" exclaimed his sister, as she snatched the teapot from his hand.

"Don't touch him. I'll call my uncle; he'll make him move," said Jessie, moving towards the door.

She was too late; Emily's act had roused the fiery temper of the boy. Placing his hands on each side of his chair, he leaned back, and lifting up his feet to the edge of the table, kicked it over and sent the tea-set crashing to the floor.

"Oh dear! Oh dear! He has broken my nice tea-set all to pieces!" cried Jessie, pausing, gazing on the wreck, and bursting into tears.

The crash of the falling tea-things was heard by Uncle Morris. He entered the room with a grave face. Charlie still sat on the chair, looking surly and wicked at the ruin he had wrought.

"See what Charlie has done, Uncle!" exclaimed Jessie, sobbing. "I wouldn't care if it wasn't poor Aunt Lucy's present that he has broken."

Aunt Lucy was dead. She had given this charming little tea-set to Jessie only a few weeks before her death.

"How did he do it?" asked Mr. Morris.

"He kicked the table over, Sir, because we wanted him to let Jessie sit in her place, and pour out the tea," said Carrie.

Just then Mrs. Carlton, and Mary the waiting-maid, both of whom had heard the noise, entered the parlor. Turning to the latter, Mr. Morris said:

"Mary, put that ugly boy to bed!"

Charlie, frightened at Mr. Morris's manner, yielded to this command without a word, and was led out of the room.

"I didn't know that so much ugliness could be got into so small a parcel before that boy came here. He goes home to-morrow morning, however, and we shall all witness his departure, I guess, with very dry eyes," said Mr. Morris.

"He needs somebody to weep over him, though, brother," interposed Mrs. Carlton, "for otherwise he will grow up into a very wicked and dangerous manhood."

"Very true, sister. He is a spoiled child. I must write to sister Hannah about him. If rigid training, and the rod of correction, be not soon applied to him, he will become a spoiled man."

After telling Mrs. Carlton the cause of this disaster, the girls with her aid began to repair the ruin wrought by ugly Charlie. Having replaced the table, they picked up the pieces, and were relieved to find that, with the exception of the knob of the teapot lid, and the handles of two cups, which were off, nothing was broken. Uncle Morris said he had a cement with which he could fasten on the knob and the handles. This relieved Jessie very much. She smiled, and said :

"Oh, I am so glad! I want to keep that tea-set, for dear Aunt Lucy's sake."

Of course the tea was all spilled, and the food scattered over the carpet. These, however, were soon replaced from the well-supplied closets of the kitchen and dining-room. In half an hour, the table was reset, and the three girls were seated, quietly eating their supper.

Did they enjoy their feast? A little, perhaps, but the upsetting of the table could not be forgotten. It chilled their spirits, and checked the flow of their joy. Thus, as always, did the evil conduct of one wrong-doer, act, like a cloud in the path of the sun, on the joy of others.

Carrie Sherwood left early in the evening, and Jessie went to her chamber with Emily to assist her in packing her trunk, so that she might be ready for an early start in the mornii g. When the last stray article was nicely packed, Emily threw herself back in the big arm-chair, and with a long-drawn sigh, ex claimed :

"Oh dear!"

"What's the matter?" inquired Jessie.

"Oh! nothing. Only I'm glad I'm going home."

"So am I," was the *thought* that leaped to Jessie's lips. She was, however, too polite to utter it, and too sincere to say she was sorry, so she sat still and said nothing.

Several minutes were passed in silence, a very unusual thing, I believe, where the company is composed of young ladies. But Jessie did not know what to say, and Emily was thinking, and did not wish to say any thing. At last she looked up and said :

"Jessie, I'm afraid I haven't behaved well since I came to Glen Morris."

Jessie again thought with Emily, and again her politeness and sincerity kept her silent. Emily went on.

"You have been very kind to me and

Charlie. I'm sorry we haven't made ourselves more agreeable to you."

"Oh ! never mind that," said Jessie. "I hope you will come and see me again, one of these days."

Emily then went on to tell Jessie about her thoughts and feelings. She had not forgotten the advice of Uncle Morris, nor had Jessie's example been without its influence over her. True, her old habits of self-will and falsehood, had acted the part of tyrants over her. Yet she had been secretly wishing to be like Jessie. These wishes, frail as they had proved themselves to be, showed that good seed from Jessie's example had been sown in her heart. Now that she was about to return home, all her better feelings were awake, and she begged forgiveness of her cousin, promising to do her best, hereafter, to be a good, truthful, affection-ate girl.

All this and much more, she said to Jessie, before they slept that night. These confessions and purposes did Emily good. They also cheered Jessie, by causing her to hope that after all, she might be to her cousin, what Guy had been to Richard Duncan.

The next morning, directly after breakfast, the hack drove up to the door, and the cousins were borne away to the depot in care of Mr. Carlton. As the carriage left the lawn, Uncle Morris patted his niece on the head, and said :

"As vinegar to the teeth, and smoke to the eyes, so are self-willed guests to those who entertain them."

"O Uncle Morris!" exclaimed Jessie, with an air of mock gravity, which showed that, harsh as her uncle's remark sounded, she felt its justice. In fact, the departure of the ungracious cousins was to the inmates of Glen Morris, like the flight of the angry storm-cloud to a company of mariners, after weary weeks of squalls and tempests.

# CHAPTER IX.

"I'm glad they are gone, and yet I'm sorry. Em seemed sorry to go, and she cried when I kissed her good-by. I really think Em loves me after all; and if it wasn't for that ugly Charlie, she would be a nice girl. But that Charlie! Oh dear! I don't think there is another such boy anywhere. I don't wonder my uncle compares him to a burr, a sting-nettle, and a hedgehog. I'm sure he's been nothing but a plague to everybody, ever since he came here. I'm glad *he's* gone, anyhow. And yet, poor fellow, I pity him. He must be miserable himself, or he wouldn't torment everybody else so—but I must go to work, I s'pose."

Thus did Jessie talk to herself, after seeing her cousins off. She had returned to the parlor, and seated herself in her small rocking-chair.

She now drew the two pieces of cloth for her
uncle's slippers, from her work-basket, and after handling them awhile with a languid air,
put them in her lap, sighed, and said—

"Oh dear! I do wish these slippers were done.
This is a hard pattern, and it will take me ever
so many days to finish it. Heigho! I 'most
wish I hadn't begun them. Let me see if I
have worsted enough to finish them."

Here Jessie leaned over and began to explore
the tangled depths of her work-basket. It was
a complete olio. Old letters, pieces of silk, velvet, linen, and woollen, scraps of paper, leaves
of books, old cords and rusty tassels, spools of
cotton, skeins of thread and knots,—in short,
almost every thing that could by any sort of
chance, or mischance, get into a young lady's
work-basket, was there in rare confusion.
Jessie's love of order was not very large. Her
temper was often sorely tried by the trouble
which her careless habit caused her when seeking a pair of scissors, or a spool of cotton. It
was so to-day. She plunged her hand deep into
the basket, in search of the colored worsteds

required for her uncle's slippers.  After feeling round awhile, she drew forth a tangled
mess, which she placed on her lap.

"Oh dear!" she said, in a complaining tone;
"how these worsteds are tangled!"

Nimbly her fingers wrought, however, and
very soon the skeins were all laid out on her
knee.

'Let me see," said she, looking at her pattern; "there are one, two, three, four—five—
six colors, and I have only one, two, three, four,
five.  Which is missing?  Ah, I see: there
is no *brown*.  Must I hunt that basket again?
It's a regular jungle—no, not a *jungle*—a jungle is a forest, mostly covered with reeds and
bushes.  This is a, a—a *jumble*.  Uncle, would
call it a basket of confusion.  Ha! ha!"

Vainly did Jessie explore her "basket of confusion."  In vain did she upset its contents upon the floor, and  replace them by handfuls.
The missing skein of brown worsted could not
be found.  At last, with wearied neck, and
aching head, she threw herself back in her chair,
and said—

" It's no use, there is no brown worsted there. But what's that?"

In leaning back, Jessie's eyes were arrested by a new book which was on the mantle. Starting from her chair, she took down the book. It was a story-book that Guy had borrowed of his friend Richard Duncan. The pictures were beautiful, and Jessie, charmed by the promise of its opening pages, gave herself up to the leadings of her excited curiosity, and soon forgot all about worsted, slippers, cousins, and uncle. Little Impulse the wizard had baited his trap with a choice book, and Jessie was in his power again.

"Why, Guy! what brought you home so early?" asked Jessie, more than two hours later, when her brother's entrance broke her attention from the book.

"Early!" exclaimed Guy, looking at his watch; "do you call fifteen minutes past twelve early?"

"Fifteen minutes past twelve!" cried Jessie, in great surprise; "it can't be so late: your watch must be wrong, Guy."

"Then the village clock is wrong, for I timed my watch by it as I came past," said Guy. "I guess you have been asleep, Sis, and didn't notice how time passed."

"Asleep, indeed! do you think I go to sleep in the morning? not I. But I've been reading your book, and was just finishing it when you came in. It's real interesting," said Jessie.

"Yes, it's a nice book," replied Guy, as he left the room in response to a call from Hugh, who was in the hall.

Jessie replaced the book, and sighed as she picked up the worsteds from the floor, to think that she had done nothing to the slippers that morning. However, as there was yet over half an hour to spare before dinner, and as she could go on with her work for the present, without the brown worsted, she began plying her needle with right good will.

Presently Uncle Morris came in. He had been out all the morning. Seeing his niece so busy, he smiled, and said:

"Busy as the bee, eh, Jessie? Well, it's the working bee that makes the honey. Guess the

little wizard has lost heart now he has found out
that my little puss has a strong will to do right,
and a strong Friend to help her."

Jessie blushed and sighed, She was in what
young Duncan would call a "tight place." She
knew that her uncle was mistaken; that she did
not deserve his praise, that by being silent she
should, of her own accord, confirm his mistake and thereby deceive him. And yet, it was
hard to confess her fault, under the circumstances. What could Jessie do?

At first she was silent. Her uncle perceiving
by her manner that something puzzled and
pained her, turned to his chair, and without
saying another word took up the morning's
newspaper and began reading.

The longer Jessie kept up his false impression, the worse she felt. Very soon, however,
the voice of the Good Spirit within her gained
the victory, and throwing the slipper into the
basket, she rose, saying to herself, "I will tell
him all about it."

Going to her uncle's side, she threw an arm
round his neck, gently drew his head towards

her and kissed him. Then she smiled through a mist of tears, and said :

"Uncle, the little wizard hasn't left Glen Morris, yet."

"Hasn't he?" replied her uncle. "Why, I thought you pricked him so sorely with your quilt needle that he had run off to Greenland, or to some other distant land to escape your little ladyship's anger, or to woo Miss Persever-ance to be his bride."

"I wish he had," sighed Jessie ; "but I fear he never will go. I wish he didn't like Glen Morris so well."

Then the little girl told her uncle how Guy's book had lured her into the wizard's power.

"Never mind, my child," said Uncle Morris, patting her head as he spoke, "never mind. Never give up. Attack him again with your tiny spear. Resolve that you will yet conquer him, as little David did big Goliah, in the name of the Lord. A little girl can be what she wills to be, if she only wills in the name of Him who is the teacher and the friend of children."

"I'll try, Uncle," said Jessie, with the fire of resolution kindling in her eyes.

" Heaven bless you, my child!" said the old man solemnly, as he placed his hands softly upon her head.   " May you always be as frank and truthful as you have now been in confessing a fault to me which you must have been very strongly tempted to conceal.   May Heaven bless you !"

Didn't Jessie feel glad then !   She was glad she had resisted the temptation to receive praise she did not merit; glad she had done right; glad her uncle was pleased with her.   Happy Jessie !   Had she by silence deceived her uncle, she would have felt guilty and ashamed.   Now she was as peaceful and hopeful as love and duty could make her.

After dinner, seeing Guy take his cap as if in great haste, Jessie followed him to the door and said:   " What makes you in such a hurry, every day, Guy?   You have not stayed to talk to me for ever so long."

" You have had company, you know, Jessie, and havn't wanted me," replied Guy, evasively

"But I have no company to-day," said Jessie. "Come, don't go yet, there's a dear, good Guy. Come into the parlor and tell me a story."

"Not now," replied Guy, opening the door. Then after a moment or two of silent thought, he shut the door and said, "If you will put on your cloak and hood I'll take you with me."

"Oh, good, good!" exclaimed the little girl; and after running to her mother for consent, she soon returned fitly equipped for a walk on that breezy November afternoon.

It being Wednesday and no school, Guy had the afternoon before him. He led his sister towards the village, telling her he was going to take her to see a good old lady of whom, he said, he was very fond.

"Who is she? How did you find her out? Does Uncle Morris know her?" were among the many questions which Jessie put to her brother. He did not see fit to satisfy her, however, except to say, "Her name is Mrs. MONEYPENNY"

"Mrs. Moneypenny! What a funny name?" exclaimed Jessie, laughing and repeating the name.

"Yes, it is odd; but the lady who bears it, is a noble woman."

"Is she rich?"

"No, she is very poor, very poor indeed."

"Very poor, eh? But how came you to know her?"

"That's my secret."

"A secret! Please tell me about it, Guy?"

"Can't do it, Jessie. You know girls can't keep secrets," replied Guy, laughing and looking archly at his sister.

"I can, Guy. Do tell me. I won't tell Hugh, nor Carrie Sherwood, no, nor even Uncle Morris, though I can't see why you should keep a secret from him."

Just then Guy and his sister were passing some open lots in the village street. Several rough boys were standing round a small bonfire which they had made out of the dead branches and leaves of trees, which the fall winds had scattered over the streets and open lots. As soon as they saw Guy, one of them cried in a jeering tone:

"There goes Mrs. Moneypenny's cow-boy!"

10

"Wonder how much he gets a week," shouted another boy.

"Perhaps he's gwine to be the old lady's
heir," said the first.

"Guess he 'spects young Jack Moneypenny's
gwine to die, down in the Brooklyn hospital,
and he wants the old ooman to adopt him.
He! he!" said a third speaker.

Loud peals of derisive laughter followed these
remarks.  Guy made no reply, but grasping his
sister's hand more tightly, he hurried past at a
rapid walk, and was soon out of hearing.

"Oh! I am so glad we are past those wicked
boys," said Jessie, slightly shivering with fear.
"But what did they call you a cow-boy for,
Guy?"

"I suppose I must tell you my secret now,"
said Guy.  "Those boys have partly let my cat
out of the bag."

Guy then told his sister, that Mrs. Moneypenny was a poor widow, with a son named
Jack.  She rented a cottage and a little piece
of land.  A cow, a few hens, and Jack's labor,
were all she had to depend upon.  Jack, being

a steady boy, earned enough to keep them comfortable in their simple way of living. But a great misfortune had overtaken them. Jack, while in Brooklyn, with a lot of eggs and chickens, which he had taken in to sell, had been knocked down and run over by a horse and wagon. His leg was broken, and he was carried to the hospital.

This sad news was quickly sent to Jack's mother. Poor old lady! It seemed as if her only stay was broken by this disaster. Being lame, she could not go to her son, neither could she take care of her cow at home. She was in deep distress, and wept many tears over poor Jack's sufferings, and her own hard fate.

Guy happened to hear her case talked over at the post-office, the very day the news of Jack's misfortune arrived. He heard a gentleman say, that she must be sent to the almshouse, though, being a woman of spirit, he feared she would break her heart and die, if she was. Full of pity for the old lady, Guy went to her, and offered to take care of her cow and hens, as long as Jack might be sick.

"It would have melted your heart" said Guy, as he finished his story, "had you seen the old lady cry for joy at my offer. She looked so thankful, and seemed so much relieved, that I felt as happy as an angel, to think that by doing such a little thing as milking and feeding a cow for a few weeks, I could shed so much light in the dwelling of a poor, but noble woman."

Jessie's eyes swam with tears. She pressed Guy's hand, but spoke not. He understood the meaning of that pressure. He knew that in her heart she was saying, "My brother did right, and those boys were very wicked for calling after him. I love my dear brother better than ever."

While such thoughts as these were passing in Jessie's mind, and Guy was feeling the gladness which welled up within him like living water, they reached the cottage. Mrs. Moneypenny received them with smiles of welcome. She kissed Jessie, and said:

"You look as if you had a heart as kind as your brother's. May Heaven bless you both!"

MRS. MONEYPENNY READING JACK'S LETTER.　　Page 155.

Then the old lady began to talk about her "dear Jack." After telling them he was "getting along nicely," she read a letter which he made out to write in pencil, as he lay bolstered up in his bed. Having finished it, the good mother sighed, and said:

"Dear Jack! How I do wish he could be brought home, so that I could take care of him myself! There is no nurse like a mother. The poor fellow says he wants some more shirts sent him, but I havn't another to send him, nor any thing to make him one with. Ah, my children, poverty is not a pleasant heritage; but never mind; life is short, and I and my poor Jack will have mansions, robes, and riches in the better land. May you, my children, be blessed with such treasures both here and hereafter!"

After Guy had "looked to the cow," in the hovel which answered for a barn, he and his sister took their leave of the widow.

Jessie walked quietly home, looking very grave, and scarcely speaking a word by the way. Once she turned to Guy and asked:

"How large a boy is Jack?"

"About my size," replied Guy.

Jessie had a big thought in her head—I mean a big thought for a little girl. If you wish to know what it was, you must consult the next chapter.

# CHAPTER X.

## MADGE CLIFTON.

WHEN Jessie reached home she threw her hood and cloak carelessly on to the floor. The cloak-stand was pretty well filled up, and she was in too much haste, to take the pains needed to find a place on the hooks for her garments. This was one of her faults. A new impulse had seized her, and she thought of nothing else. Bounding into her mother's room, she said:

"Mother, will you let me make two shirts for poor Jack Moneypenny?"

Mrs. Carlton looked up from her work, and after a moment's glance at the eager face of her daughter, asked:

"Who is Jack Moneypenny, my dear?"

Jessie, in her eagerness to carry her point, had forgotten to ask if her mother knew any thing of the widow, or her son, Jack. This question checked her ardor a little, and she told the story of the widow's misfortune. Just as she was finishing her tale, however, she thought of Guy's wish to keep his part in the affair a secret. So blushing deeply, she added:

"Oh dear! what will Guy say? I promised to keep it all secret, and now I have told all about it. He said girls couldn't keep a secret, and I believe he is right. What shall I do, Mother?"

"Why tell him that you have told me, to be sure. Guy has no secrets with his mother, and I am sure he does not wish his sister to have any."

"Has Guy told you about it, then?"

"Yes, he told me all his plans from the first. Guy never conceals any thing from his mother."

"What made you ask me who Jack Money-penny was, then, Ma, if you knew before?"

"Only to teach my Jessie, that she ought to be less abrupt in her manners. You should have stated your case first, and then have asked me your question"

"So I should, Ma," said Jessie, musing a few moments, and gazing on her foot, as she traced the outline of the carpet-pattern with it. Then, smiling, she looked up, and added, "but you knew, Mamma, it is my way, to speak first, and think afterwards."

"Not a very wise way, either," said Mrs. Carlton; "but about those shirts, why do you wish to make them?"

Jessie told her mother about Jack's letter, and what the widow had said.

"Well," replied Mrs. Carlton; "I will give you the cloth, and cut out the shirts, if you really wish to make them."

"I do, Mother, very much wish to do it. Only think how glad the widow will be, and how comfortable the shirts will make the poor sick boy, in that horrid hospital."

"Very true, my dear, but how about your uncle's slippers, and cushion, and watch-pocket?"

A blush tinged Jessie's cheek again. The little wizard had once more hurried her into a new plan before her old ones had been worked

out. Plainly she could not help poor Jack
and keep her former resolution, not to be
turned aside from finishing her gifts for Uncle
Morris. She was fairly puzzled. It was
right to make shirts for a poor boy. It was
right to keep her purposes too. Yet she could
not do both. But did not the boy need the
shirts, more than Uncle Morris did his slippers?
Would not her uncle be willing to wait? No
doubt he would, but then her promise to finish
the slippers before beginning any thing else,
was part of a plan for conquering a bad habit.
Would it be right to depart from that plan?

Such were the questions which floated like
unpleasant dreams through Jessie's mind as she
sat with her hands on the back of a chair-seat,
knocking her heels against the floor. Her
mother, though she allowed her to think awhile
in silence, read her thoughts in the workings of
her face. When Jessie seemed to be lost in the
fog of her own thoughts, Mrs. Carlton came to
her aid, and said :

" Jessie."

" Yes, Ma."

"I have been thinking that poor Jack needs those shirts directly, and that you could not make him a pair in less than two, perhaps in not less than three weeks. So I don't see how you can help him out of his present trouble."

Jessie sighed, and said, "I didn't think of that."

"Well, I have a plan to propose. I will send him two of Guy's shirts to-morrow, and you shall make two new ones for Guy, at your leisure."

"What a dear, good, nice mother you are," cried Jessie, running to Mrs. Carlton, and giving her more kisses than I am able to count.

Thus did a mother's love find a key with which to unlock Jessie's puzzle, and to enable her to help poor Jack, without breaking her purpose to finish Uncle Morris's things, and thereby drive that plague of her life, the little wizard, away from Glen Morris.

"I will work ever so hard, see if I don't, Ma," said she, as she patted her mother's check. "I will finish the slippers, and get the shirts done, too, before Christmas. Don't you think I can?"

"You *can*, I have no doubt, if you try my dear."

"Well, I'll *try* then. I'll join Guy's famous Try Company, and will try and try, and try again, until I fairly succeed."

Mrs. Carlton kissed her daughter affectionately; after which the now light-hearted girl bounded out of the room, singing—

> " If you find your case is hard,
> Try, try, try again.
> Time will bring you your reward,
> Try, try, try again.
> All that other people do,
> Why with patience should not you?
> Only keep this rule in view,
> Try, try, try again."

"That's it! That's it, my little puss," said Uncle Morris, who was in the parlor which Jessie entered singing her joyous roundelay " Corporal Try is a little fellow, but he has helped do all the great things that have ever been done. There is nothing good or great which he cannot do. He will help a little girl learn to darn her own stocking, or make a quilt for her old uncle; and he will help men build big steamships, construct railroads over the desert, or lay a telegraph wire under the waters of the ocean. Oh, a great little man is Corporal Try!"

"I know it," replied Jessie, "and I've joined his company; so if you meet little Impulse the wizard, please tell him not to come here again unless he wishes to be beaten with a big club called good resolution."

"Bravely spoken, Lady Jessie! May you never desert the Corporal's colors! Above all, may you always obtain grace from above whereby to conquer yourself, which is the grandest deed you can possibly perform."

Jessie sat down to her work-basket, and took up one of the pieces of cloth for her uncle's slippers. But as it was now late in the afternoon of a dull November day, she could not see to embroider very well. So she thought she would go out again and buy the brown worsted which was needed in working out the figure on the slippers. Going to the window first, she noticed that the sky looked cold and bleak. The wind, too, was whistling mournfully among the branches of the trees, and round the corners of the house. It was evidently going to be a cold night. Turning from the window again, she said to her brother Hugh, who was sitting very cosily in a large arm-chair before the glowing fire in the grate:

"Please, Hugh, will you run down to the village with me? I want to get some worsted at Mrs. Horton's."

"Why didn't you get it this afternoon?" asked Hugh in his usual grumpy way when asked to do any thing.

"I didn't think of it"

"Didn't think of it, eh? Well, I don't think I shall be your lackey this cold afternoon. I'd rather sit here and keep my toes warm."

"Do go, dear Hugh, please do!" said Jessie in her mellowest tones. "I shall want the worsted to-morrow morning."

"Oh, go to Greenwich! You are always wanting something. Girls want a mighty sight of waiting on. I won't go."

Jessie turned away from her ungracious brother wishing, as she had so often done, that he " was more like Guy." Had it been a little earlier in the afternoon. she would have gone alone; but as it was nearly dark she preferred company.

" Oh dear !" sighed she, " what shall I do ? I wish Guy was in."

"Perhaps you would accept an old man's company," said her uncle, rising and buttoning up his coat.

"I should be very, very glad to have it, but I don't want to trouble you, Uncle," she replied.

" It's no trouble to go out with my little puss. Besides, by going, I can give this drone-like brother of yours a practical lesson in that love and politeness which he so much despises. I shall certainly be happier going with you, than he will be in the indulgence of his selfishness before the fire."

Hugh said something in a grumbling tone which neither his uncle nor sister understood.

In a few minutes the good old man, having firm hold of Jessie's hand, was breasting the cold wind as they walked smartly along the frozen road leading to the village.

"You will have a chance to try your new skates to-morrow if it is as cold as this all night," said Mr. Morris, as they crossed the bridge over the brook.

"Won't that be nice?" replied Jessie; "Carrie Sherwood has a pair too, and we will both try together. I guess I shall get some bumps though before I learn to skate well. I wish we had some one to teach us how to use them."

"What will you give me, if I consent to be your teacher?"

"Oh, Uncle Morris! You don't mean it, do you?"

"To be sure I do. When I was young they called me the best skater in town. I could go through all kinds of movements, and even cut my name on the ice with my skates. I guess I haven't quite forgotten how I used to do it. But what will you give me if I consent to teach you?"

"I will love you ever so much, and so will Carrie."

"But I thought you loved me ever so much already?"

"Well, so I do, Uncle. I love you better than I love anybody in the world, except ma and pa. But I will love you better and better."

"That's pay enough," said Mr. Morris, warmly pressing the hand of his niece. "The pure fresh love of a child's heart is worth more to an old man like me than much gold. It makes my heart grow young again—but what have we here?"

They had now reached a stone wall which fronted the estate of Esquire Duncan. An angle in the fence had made a corner, in which was seated a girl of about Jessie's age and size. She was clothed in rags; her feet were bare. She had no covering on her head save her tangled hair. Her face and arms were brown and dirty. She shivered in the piercing wind, and traces of recent tears were visible in the dirt which covered her woe-worn face.

"Poor little girl! I wonder where she lives?" exclaimed Jessie.

"Where do you live, my dear?" asked Mr Morris, addressing the child.

"New York," replied the outcast curtly.

11

"How came you here?"

"Mother left me down yonder," said the girl, pointing to the four cross-roads just beyond.

"Where is your mother now?"

"Don't know."

"What did she say when she left you?"

"She told me to sit on the trough of the pump while she went to buy some bread. But she didn't come back, and I came over here out of the wind."

"How long since she left you?"

"Ever so long."

"Poor little girl! I'm afraid your mother brought you out here to cast you off, and so get rid of you," said Uncle Morris.

"Guess not! Guess she got drunk somewhere," said the girl, in a manner so cold and dogged that Mr. Morris shuddered.

Here, Jessie, whose eyes were swimming with tears, pulled her uncle's hand. Taking him a little aside, she said—

"Please, Uncle, take her home, and let me give her something to eat."

"Better take her to the alms-house, I'm

thinking," replied her uncle. "She may be a wicked girl."

"Then we can teach her to be good," said Jessie.

This was a home thrust that went right to the good old man's heart. "The alms-house," he thought, "is not a very likely place to grow goodness in. It is too chilly and heartless. There will be little sympathy there with the struggles and sorrows of a child like this; Jessie shall have her way this time. She shall go with us."

After forming this purpose, he looked at his niece, and said—

"Perhaps you are right, Jessie. The poor creature shall go home with us, at least, for to-night."

"Oh, I am *so* glad, I'm *so* glad," cried Jessie, clapping her hands, then running to the shivering child, who had been watching them during this conversation with a puzzled air, she said—

"Come, little girl, you are to go home with me. Uncle says so."

"I don't want to. I'll wait here for mother,"

replied the girl, shrinking back into her corner, against the rough stone wall.

"My child," said Mr. Morris, "I fear your mother has left you here on purpose, and that she will never come back. If she is in the place, you shall go to her as soon as we can find her. If you stay here you will freeze. Come with us and we will give you a supper, and let you warm yourself before a rousing fire, while we search for your mother."

The idea of supper and a rousing fire took hold of the little outcast's feelings. Gathering her rags close to her chilled body she stepped forward, and said—

"I'll go with you."

"What is your name?" inquired Jessie.

"Madge!" said the child, curtly.

"Madge what?" asked Uncle Morris.

"Madge Clifton!" said the child.

"Which means, I suppose, Margaret Clifton," said the old gentleman. "A pretty name enough, and I wish its owner was in a prettier condition. But come, let us hasten out of this cold biting wind."

Poor little, shivering Madge! Waiting so
long for her mother, alone and in a strange
place, had made her heart heavy and sad.
Her limbs were so stiff with cold she could
scarcely walk, at first. But the kind looks of
the good old gentleman, and the loving words
of Jessie, cheered her on; and in a few minutes
they entered the back door of Glen Morris Cottage.

# CHAPTER XI

"WHAT have you here, my brother?" asked Mrs. Carlton, as, in response to a message from Mr. Morris, she entered the kitchen, where poor Madge sat on a cricket before the range, looking, as Jessie afterwards said, "like a cat in a strange garret."

"She's a heap o' rags and dirt, mem," interposed the servant, who did not fancy the introduction of such an unsightly object into her prim-looking dominions.

"She is a poor, starving, and half-frozen girl, without any kind mother to take care of her and love her," said Jessie, who feared, from her mother's looks, that poor Madge was as unwelcome a guest to her, as she was to the kitchen-maid.

"She is a poor, little human waif, which has

floated to our door on a sea of trouble and misfortune, sister," observed Mr. Morris. "If *opportunity* is the gate of *duty*, then we owe it to this little girl, and to the Great Father who sent her to our doors, to relieve her wants, and if needs be, provide for her in future."

This view of her relation to poor little Madge, somewhat softened Mrs. Carlton's feelings. She was a very kind woman—in fact, she was nearly all *heart*—but she was fastidiously neat. Madge's dirt and rags had repelled her at first sight; had shut out from her thoughts, for the moment, the recollection, that within that covering of filthy rags, there sat a human creature, which, had it been loved, and taught, and trained as her own child had been, might have been as loving, and as attractive as she. Her brother's remark brought this view of Madge's case before her, but did not wholly divest her of her first feelings. Jessie's instincts led her to see that her mother was not quite prepared to take the outcast girl to her affections, and trembling for the result, she followed up her uncle's plea, by saying:

"We found her cold and hungry, sitting under a stone wall, waiting for her mother, who has run away from her. If we had not brought her home, she would have frozen to death before morning. Wouldn't that have been terrible, Ma?"

"Poor thing!" exclaimed Mrs. Carlton, her sympathy being now fully aroused, "but, Brother, why did you not take her to the almshouse, where they have the means of cleansing and clothing such unhappy outcasts?"

"Perhaps it would have been more prudent, my sister, to have done so; but I took counsel of your child's heart, and not of my own prudence. This is Jessie's *protégé*. When she pleaded in her behalf, I thought I would do for Madge, what I and you would wish another to do for Jessie, should she ever, by any sad reverse of fortune, become an outcast child."

"Halloo, what little dollymop have you got here?" cried Hugh, who, at this juncture, bounded into the kitchen to see what was going on.

"Poor little creature! She has had a hard

road to. travel, thus far, I guess," said Guy, who accompanied his brother. Hugh looked at the child's appearance only. Guy, like his uncle and Jessie, viewed her as a human being in distress.

All this time, the object of these comments, stared strangely about, looking, now at the things around her, and then into the faces of the different persons in the group. At first, she seemed indifferent to their remarks. But when Hugh called her a little dollymop, her large, black eyes flashed angrily upon him. Guy's kind words and tones disarmed her, however, and a pearl-like tear rolled down her cheeks.

"Well," said Mrs. Carlton, with a sigh of resignation to circumstances, "the poor thing is here, and must be cared for." Then turning to the servant, she added, "Take the poor child into the bath-room. Give her a thorough cleansing and combing, while I look out some of Jessie's clothes for her. Take those rags she has on, and throw them on the dirt heap!"

The party in the kitchen now broke up.

Uncle Morris, the boys, and Jessie, went into
the parlor, where they found Mr. Carlton who
had just returned from the city. ˙ He approved
of what Uncle Morris had done, but thought it
best to inquire, at once, for Madge's mother at
the village tavern. As there was yet an hour
to spare before tea, he took Guy, and started in
pursuit of the heartless mother.

Where was she? After leaving Madge at
the pump, she had gone to the tavern, and
purchased some gin. After drinking a large
glass of the fiery liquor, she put down the glass
and the money, looking so ravenously at the
sparkling decanter, that the landlord feared she
was going crazy. Reaching her skinny fingers
out towards the bottle, she said, in a screeching
voice: "Give me another glass!"

Hardly knowing what he was about, the
andlord filled her glass a second time. She
swallowed its contents at a single gulp, and de-
manded more. Alarmed at her manner the man
refused. Then her anger awoke. She poured
forth a volley of strange and fearful words.
The passers-by came in to see what was the

matter. To be rid of her tongue and to save
the reputation of his house, as he said, the landlord called in his stable-boys, and they hurled
her into the street.

There she drew upon herself the attention of
Jem Townsend and the crew of idle boys which
usually accompanied him. They gathered
round the unhappy woman, as she sat on the
edge of the curb-stone cursing the tavern-keeper,
and began to tease her.

"Fuddled, eh?" said Jem Townsend, laughing. Then he added, "What do you do here,
Lady Ginswiller? Rather a cold seat this for
a lady, eh? Better walk into old Bottlenose's
best parlor, hadn't ye?"

Upon this the poor maudlin creature cursed
louder than ever. The wicked urchins laughed
and hooted in turn, until she rose in a fit of
passion and pursued them.

The boys ran down the village street, pausing
now and then to quicken her rage by some
biting words. And thus they led her at last to
the vicinity of a low grocery. Drawn by the
scent of rum, like the vulture to its quarry, she

staggered into the grocery. laid down her last sixpence on the bar, and muttered. "Give me a drink of rum."

It was given her. She drank the wretched stuff, and reeling to the door-step, fell down insensibly drunk. What a spectacle of pity! And yet that poor, pitiable creature had once been a fair and lovely girl, as full of life and hope as she was of health and beauty. But now, alas, how fallen! What had done it? The wine cup, used in circles of fashion, began the work of ruin. Rum and gin were doing their best to finish it.

Finding they could not rouse her, the boys ran off to Mr. Tipstaff, the constable, and told him about her. That worthy repaired to the spot. Aided by one or two others he dragged her to a magistrate's office; and he sent her to jail as a common vagrant.

These facts were all told to Mr. Carlton and Guy by the landlord of the hotel, who painted the poor woman in very dark colors. After calling on the magistrate and requesting that the prisoner might be detained the next day until it was ascertained certainly that she was Madge's mother, he and Guy returned home with sad hearts. They talked the matter over as they walked. Among other questions, Guy asked:

"Do *many* women become drunkards, Pa?"

"Yes, a great many; though drunken women are not so common as drunken men, by far."

"It always makes me feel bad to see a tipsy man; but when I once saw a tipsy *woman* in New York, it made me shudder. How do *women* learn to drink, Pa? They don't go to the tavern like men, do they?"

"Not at first, Guy. Usually they begin at home, or at parties, or when stopping at the great hotels, where wine is drunk at the dinner-table. In many families, also, wine is used at the table, and fathers and mothers teach their daughters to drink it as a daily beverage. But generally, I believe, ladies begin their habit of drinking wine at parties, taking it, at first, not from choice, but because they don't like to be thought singular."

"But I don't see how drinking a little wine

at a party can teach a lady to be a drunkard, Pa," remarked Guy.

"It does not do so, my son, in every case. But too often a lady will acquire an appetite for wine, which gradually grows stronger and stronger until she cannot control it. This appetite is not awakened in all who drink, but it *may* be. Hence, it is better for all, boys, girls, men, and women, not to touch the drink that is in the drunkard's bowl."

"So I think, Pa," said Guy, "and therefore, I mean to be a tee-totaler as long as I live."

"That's right, my son. It is always best to keep as far from a dangerous place as possible."

When Mr. Carlton and Guy reached home, tea was ready, and they went at once to the cheerful table. Jessie could scarcely wait while the blessing was asked, so impatient was she to know if Madge's mother had been found. As soon, therefore, as Uncle Morris ceased speaking, she broke forth and said :

"O Pa! you don't know how nice Madge will look when she is washed and dressed. Please tell me if you have seen her mother ?"

"No, I have not *seen* her," replied her father, smiling.

Jessie's face brightened. She had been fearing that Madge would have to go away if her mother was found. Looking archly at her father, she said—

"I'm *so* glad. *Now* poor Madge can stay here!"

"Why, Jessie, you surprise me," said Mrs. Carlton. "Is it any thing to be glad about, that a little girl has lost her mother?"

With a blush mantling her cheek: the little girl exclaimed—

"Her mother is a wicked woman, Ma, and don't make her happy, nor teach her to be good. If Madge has lost her, and you let her live with us and be a mother to her, she will be a good deal better off, and much happier than she could be with her own mother."

"Spoken like a philosopher!" exclaimed Uncle Morris. "The loss of a drunken mother is not, indeed, a thing to mourn over, especially if that loss brings with it the gain of a home in which Love is the perpetual Preside t—but I suspect from your pa's looks that Madge's mother is not wholly lost, yet."

" *Why!* didn't pa say he couldn't find her ?" said Jessie, looking with a puzzled air at her father.

"Not exactly, my dear," replied Mr. Carlton. " I said I had not *seen* her, which is true ; but I have *heard* of her, as I suppose ; for a strange woman did go to the tavern about the time Madge was left, and is now in jail as a drunken vagrant."

" Oh, how shocking !" exclaimed Jessie.

Mr. Carlton now told all he had heard about the supposed Mrs. Clifton, and it was agreed that Uncle Morris should see her in the morning and learn if she was, indeed, the poor child's mother.

After tea, Jessie hurried to the kitchen to look after her *protégé*. She found her so changed by her washing and new dress, that notwithstanding her high expectations, she could hardly believe her to be the same Madge she had seen sitting there an hour before. But Madge it was, as bright and good-looking a girl as could be found anywhere, in or out of Duncanville.

"Have you had enough to eat, Madge?" inquired Jessie, scarcely knowing how to act the part of an agreeable hostess.

"Indade, miss, but she has eaten more like a hungry pig than a gal," said Mary, before Madge had time to reply.

Jessie could not keep from laughing at Mary's not very complimentary comparison. Hence, she turned her head so as not to hurt the little girl's feelings. As soon as she could make her face straight and sober again, she sat down beside Madge, and taking her hand, said—

"Would you like to see my doll?"

But Madge had other and higher thoughts than of dolls or playthings. She was in a sort of wonder-world. She could not satisfy herself with regard to the meaning of the change brought about in her during the last hour or two. That pleasant kitchen, the neat dress she wore, the bath by which she had been cleansed from the filth of poverty, the pleasant faces she

12

had seen, and the kind voices she had heard, all seemed to her like a gay dream, and she was expecting, ay, and fearing too, that the next minute she should awake and find herself sitting and shivering in the cold wind, under the stone wall, waiting for her ungentle mother. But when Jessie touched her hand and spoke so kindly to her, every thing seemed real, and her heart sent up gushes of gratitude to the little friend who, like some good fairy, had conjured away her rags, and pain, and cold, and hunger. After gazing silently into Jessie's eyes a few moments, as if she was trying to look into her soul, she said—

"Little girl, will you let me love you?"

"To be sure I will, and I will love *you* too," replied Jessie, in tones that seemed like angel's music to the little outcast, whose ears had long been unfamiliar with loving words.

Then Jessie threw an arm round Madge and pressing her to her bosom, gave her a kiss. Oh, how warmly did the outcast girl return it! She clung to Jessie as the wild vine does to the supporting branch, and embraced her with an ardor which told more eloquently than words could utter it, how grateful she was for the love which Jessie had offered her.

When Madge withdrew her arms from Jessie, she sat back in her chair and gazed at her long and silently. After a time the tears filled her eyes, and in broken accents she asked—

".Does any one know where my mother is?"

Jessie told her she was probably in the village, and that she would, most likely, see her in the morning. Madge begged hard to be taken to her that night, but was finally persuaded to wait until the morrow.

"That child has a great deal of *heart*," said Uncle Morris, after hearing Jessie's account of her interview with Madge. "We must do what we can to rescue her from the influence of her drunken mother."

# CHAPTER XII.

## LITTLE IMPULSE BEATEN AGAIN.

AFTER breakfast the next morning, Jessie sat down to her work with a resolute will. Her *impulse*, was to spend the hours playing with Madge. But her purpose to act by rule was strong, and it conquered. Guy went out for the brown worsted, which her meeting with Madge, kept her from buying the previous evening. So giving her *protégé* a seat on a cricket by her side, she worked merrily, and with nimble fingers, on her uncle's slippers. The tongues of the two girls, you may be sure, were as nimble as Jessie's fingers.

While they were thus happily employed, Uncle Morris was out, looking after the young outcast's mother.

Jessie had not been seated more than an hour before her brother Hugh, with his friend,

Walter Sherwood and his sister Carrie, came in, each armed with a pair of skates, and well wrapped up, as was fitting they should be, on a cold day in November. Carrie bounded into the room like a fawn, and kissing her friend, exclaimed:

"O Jessie! this is a capital morning for skating! Walter has found a nice safe place, and we have come to take you with us."

This was a strong temptation. Perhaps a stronger could not have been offered, to incline her to break her purpose, and drop her work. There had been no day since her skates had been given her, in which there had been ice enough to try them. It was a new amusement, too, and her heart was set upon it. Hence, an impulse came over her, to pitch the slipper into the basket, seize her skates, and hurry away to the desired spot. In fact, she half rose from the chair, and words of consent were rising to her lips, when she thought of the little wizard, and reseating herself, replied:

"I would like to go ever so much, Carrie, but I must stay in until dinner-time, and work on uncle's slippers."

"Bother the slippers! Who cares about them! Uncle don't need them, and why should you be fussing over them," said Hugh.

"It's very pleasant to work for your good old uncle, I dare say, Miss Jessie, but you can do that in the afternoon. We very much wish you to join our party this morning," observed Walter.

"I know I *could*," replied Jessie; "but mother wishes me to sew or study every morning until dinner-time, and I have resolved to do it. I have broken my purpose a great many times, but I *must* keep it now, much as I want to go out skating. Can't you put off your party until the afternoon?"

"Not a bit of it!" said Hugh. "Come Walt, come Carrie, let us be off."

"I think I will stay with Jessie this morning," replied Carrie; "and I invite you, young gentlemen, to beau us to the skating-ground, this afternoon!"

"If you won't go now, you may beau yourselves for all we," retorted Hugh in his usual ungracious way, when treating with his sister.

"Don't say *so*, Hugh," responded Walter. "It's hardly polite. 'Spose you and I go without the girls this morning, and *with* them this afternoon? Eh?"

"As you please!" growled Hugh, swinging his skates; "only let us be off quick."

The boys now left, promising to go with the girls at half-past two in the afternoon. Carrie laid aside her hood and cloak, which Jessie took, and laid in a heap upon the table.

"My dear!" observed Mrs. Carlton, who looked into the room just at that moment; "is *that* the place for Carrie's things?"

A blush tinged Jessie's cheek. As I have said before, a want of regard for order, was a fault which grew out of her impulsive nature. She did most things in a hurry, and usually with some other object before her mind at the same time. While her uncle had been trying to cure her of the habit of yielding to her impulses, her mother had also been endeavoring to stimulate her to cultivate a love of order. No wonder, then, that she blushed as she went to hang her friend's hood and cloak on the stand in the hall.

All this time, poor Madge had sat almost unnoticed. So taken up were they all with their skating party, that they had overlooked the quiet maiden, sitting so demurely on her cricket. But now the boys were gone, and the two friends took their seats, Jessie's thoughts came back to the young outcast, and turning to Carrie, she said:

"Carrie, let me introduce you to Madge Clifton."

"How do you do, miss?" said Carrie, bowing.

Poor Madge did not know much about introductions, and was unused to company. So she only blushed, hung down her head, and replied:

"Pretty well, thank ye."

Jessie now took Carrie aside, and in whispers told her poor Madge's story, after which they resumed their seats. Carrie's warm heart soon melted away the poor outcast's fears; and while the two young ladies were merrily prattling away, Madge listened with wonder if not with delight. In fact, her life since last evening seemed more like a dream than a reality to her. She was still in fairy-land.

Presently the postman came to the house bringing a letter addressed to "Miss Jessie Carlton." The servant took it to Jessie on a small salver.

' Is it for me?" cried Jessie, taking it up and examining the address.

"Whom can it be from?" asked Carrie, leaning over to her friend's side to see the handwriting.

"Oh, I know!" exclaimed Jessie. "It's from cousin Emily."

The letter was opened, and Jessie read aloud as follows:

MORRISTOWN, N. J., November 18, 18—.

MY DEAR JESSIE:

I got home nicely from your house. Ma was very glad to see us, and so was pa. Charlie said he was glad to get home. I was some glad and some sorry. It was pleasant to see pa and ma again, but I missed you, oh! ever so much! When I went up to my room that night, I sat down and cried. I thought over all the naughty things I had said and done

to you while 'I was at Glen Morris, until it
seemed to me I was the most wicked girl in the
world. I thought of you and of dear Uncle
Morris and his good advice, until my heart
seemed broken. Then I kneeled down and
asked God to make me a good girl like you. I
begin to believe he will, for I have been trying
hard to be good ever since. Mother says I am
a very good girl already; but she don't know
what passes in my thoughts, nor how hard I
have to strive to keep down my ugly, wicked
temper. Charlie is not quite so wicked as he
was, either, and I am trying to make him a
good boy. I wish you would come to Morristown and make me a good long visit. With
much love to yourself, and your good Ma, Pa,
and Uncle Morris, I am

                Your affectionate cousin,

                        EMILY MORRIS.

To MISS JESSIE CARLTON.


"What a beautiful letter!" said Carrie.

Jessie was silent. She was thinking. She
was secretly rejoicing, too. Such a joy was in

her young heart as had never welled up in it before. She had done Emily good. As Guy had led Richard Duncan into right paths, so she had led Emily. Happy, happy Jessie!

Just then she heard Uncle Morris's night-key lifting the latch of the hall door. Away she bounded from her seat, almost overturning poor Madge in her hurry. Rushing to her uncle as he was closing the door, she seized his arm with one hand while she held up Emily's letter in the other, and in a loud, earnest whisper, said:

"O Uncle! Cousin Emily is trying to be good. She says so in her letter."

Uncle Morris stooped to imprint a kiss on the upturned lips of the eager child. Then patting her head gently, he said:

"It is not every sower of good seed that finds his harvest sheaf so quickly as you have done. Perhaps the Great Husbandman has given my Jessie hers to encourage her to sow, and sow, and sow again—but Jessie, I have found your Madge's mother."

"Have you, *truly?*" asked Jessie, feeling her interest suddenly revived in her *protégé.*

"Yes. Come with me to your mother's room and I will tell you all about it."

This "mother's room" was up-stairs, and up they went. Finding Mrs. Carlton there with her seamstress, they sat down, and Uncle Morris told his story. Said he:

"I have seen Mrs. Clifton. She is sober this morning, and is quite a well-bred, intelligent woman. She has been respectable; was well married to a reputable man. But foolishly forsaking their quiet country home, they went to the city in the hope of acquiring property. There her husband, failing to get work, took to drinking and died. Mrs. Clifton buried him, and, dreading to go back to her old home because of poverty, tried to support herself by needlework. In an evil hour she took to drinking; first as a stimulant to labor, and then as a cordial to soothe her griefs. Of course she soon sank very low, and made poor Madge go out to beg. At last, stung with remorse, she resolved to quit the city, and, seeking work in the country, become a sober woman again. Filled with this purpose she travelled as far as Duncânville with her child, when her appetite for drink came upon her. Leaving Madge at the Four Corners she sought the tavern. The rest you know. *We* found the child, and *she* spent the night in the lock-up."

" Poor thing !" exclaimed Mrs. Carlton.

"Poor little Madge !" cried Jessie, who very naturally felt more for the unfortunate child, than for the unhappy, but guilty mother.

" Yes," said Mr. Morris, " but pity alone won't do them much good. The question is, what shall be done with them ?"

"True," rejoined Mrs. Carlton, " but are you sure the woman's story is true ?"

"It agrees with the account Madge gave of herself, so far as the affair of last evening is concerned. Being true in *one* thing, I hope it is in all. She has, however, given me references to her old friends in the country, and professes to be very anxious to live a reformed life. I will write to her friends, but, mean-while, what shall we do with her ?"

" Let her come here, and stay with Madge ?" suggested Jessie.

Mrs. Carlton looked at her brother, and read in his eyes an approval of her daughter's suggestion.

"Be it so," said she, "if you think best. I can keep her busy with her needle, until we hear from her friends, and something offers Perhaps a few days spent in our quiet home, will confirm her in her feeble purposes to re-enter the way of sobriety."

"Spoken just like yourself!" said Mr. Morris, with an expression which showed how greatly he loved and admired his sister. "I will go after the poor creature directly."

"Oh, I'm *so* glad Madge's mother is coming here to live!" cried Jessie, clapping her hands, and running down-stairs to tell the good news to her *protégé*.

The outcast child looked a gratitude she did not know how to express, after hearing what Jessie had to say. She fixed her large, black eyes, swimming in tears, upon her friendly hostess, and silently watched her every mo-tion.

"I think it's very kind of your mother, to

take a stranger into her house so," whispered Carrie.

"So it is," replied Jessie, who was now busy with her embroidery on the slipper. "So it is, but my Uncle Morris says that it is godlike to be kind, and that if we are kind and loving to poor people, the great God will honor us, and care for us."

Carrie looked at the sweet face of Jessie with admiration for some time, without saying a word. At last, to break the silence, she said:

"Won't we have a good time, skating this afternoon?"

"I hope so," said Jessie; "and we will take Madge with us, shall we?"

"Can you skate, Madge?" asked Carrie.

Madge shook her head. The child was nervous and uneasy about the coming of her mother. She was afraid she might come to the house tipsy, and so offend the friends who loved her so well.

"Can you *slide* on the ice?" asked Jessie.

"Yes, ma'am," replied Madge, evidently getting to be more and more absent-minded.

"She is thinking about her mother," whis
pered Carrie.

"Yes, don't let us trouble her," replied
Jessie.

Quickly sped the bright needle, with its
beautiful worsteds, along the slipper, and quickly grew into shape the flowers which were to
form the pattern. A happy heart and a resolute
will, make her fingers both nimble and skilful.

By and by, Uncle Morris's night-key was
heard opening the door-latch again. Jessie
started, listened a moment, then dropped her
work, and taking Madge's hand, said:

"Your mother is come!"

"Where is she?" asked the child, looking
anxiously toward the door.

"Come with me, I'll show you," said Jessie,
taking her by the hand.

They went into the hall. Uncle Morris was
there, and so was Mrs. Clifton. She was a
short, slender, well-formed woman, with large,
dark bloodshot eyes. Her face was pale, her
cheeks hollow, and her hair uncombed. She
was poorly dressed, and yet there was some

thing about her, which told of better things
As soon as she saw Madge, she ran to her,
folded her nervously to her bosom, and exclaimed:

"Oh! my child! pity your poor, wretched
mother!"

Madge, finding her mother to be sober, grew
cheerful. Her mother, after being taken to the
bath-room, and furnished with some changes of
raiment, was installed in the room with the
seamstress, and then, as waters close up, and
flow on smoothly again, after a little disturb-
ance, so did affairs at Glen Morris move on
once more, in their wonted quiet course.

13

# CHAPTER XIII.

## The Skating Party.

"Now you can go skating with me, can't you?" inquired Carrie Sherwood, as she pushed her little round face in at the door after dinner.

"Yes, *now* I can go," replied Jessie. "I did ever so much on my slipper this morning, and shall get it done by the last of the week."

"If you stick to it, but I know you *won't*," said Hugh, interrupting his sister.

Jessie felt a little anger stir in her heart on hearing this fling at a habit she was trying so so hard to overcome. But saying to herself, "never mind, I deserve it," she merely gave Hugh a glance of reproof, and was silent.

"I say, that's ungenerous, Mister Hugh," observed Guy, taking up his sister's case. "You know Jessie is learning to stick to her purposes, and that is more than anybody can say of you."

"Don't be too hard upon a fellow just for a joke," replied Hugh, wincing under his brother's hit.

"Well, don't you throw stones at Jessie; at least, not so long as you live in a glass house yourself," said Guy. Then turning to the girls, he added: "Come girls, get ready, and I'll go with you to help Jessie try her new skates."

"Oh, thank you, you dear good Guy!" replied Jessie, running to her brother and giving him a sweet sisterly kiss.

"I think I'll go, too, if you'll let me," said Hugh.

"You may if you'll promise not to poke fun at us if we fall down," replied Jessie.

"If you do poke fun, master Hugh," said Carrie, shaking her head at him, "we will never consent to let you join our party again!"

"That will be *terrible!*" exclaimed Hugh, with mock gravity. "Why I'd rather be drummed out of our Archery club than be turned off by the ladies."

"Well, you may go this time, if you will carry my skates," said Jessie.

"Of course I will; and is there any thing else, in the small way, that your most humble servant can do for you?" asked Hugh, bowing almost to the ground.

A laugh greeted this act of mock humility, and then all parties prepared to face the keen breeze in search of recreation on the ice.

"Where is Madge? is she ready?" shouted Jessie, as she stood at the foot of the stairs, warmly muffled for her walk.

"Yes, Miss, here she is," replied Madge's mother, as she came to the top of the stairs, leading her daughter by the hand.

Madge was dressed in an old plaid cloak, which had become too small for Jessie, and in a scarlet hood which had been laid aside for the same reason.

"A regular little red riding-hood, isn't she?" whispered Hugh, to his brother, after taking a survey of the prim, little black-eyed miss before him. Then looking sour and angry, he added

"But why does Jessie take the beggar's brat out with her?"

"Hugh! Hugh! Don't talk in that way," replied Guy, putting his hand playfully over his brother's mouth.

"Get out!" cried Hugh, pushing his brother's hand away and walking off in high dudgeon, in search of Walter, who, for some reason, had not come with his sister. His foolish pride had kindled anger in his breast.

Madge, with the usual quickness of girls of her age, had caught enough of Hugh's words, and of the meaning of his act, to perceive that he was disposed to treat her with scorn. A cloud flitted across her brow, and her eyes flashed. It was clear that the proud, thoughtless boy had wounded her feelings.

"Hugh! Hugh! Don't carry off my skates!" shouted Jessie, as her brother turned into the main road, from the lawn.

Whirling the skates over the fence, he kept on without a word. The skates, fortunately, fell on a heap of dry leaves and were picked up uninjured by Guy, who, with the three girls,

soon found the way to some hollows, in the pas
ture, near the brook. These hollows, filled
with shallow pools of water, now solidly frozen,
were excellent places for young misses to slide
and skate in.

Madge was not cheerful this afternoon.
Hugh had wounded her pride, and stirred her
sleeping passions. It was very ungenerous conduct, in a lad of his age, to treat an unfortunate
child with scorn. Madge ought not to have
allowed her · temper to be ruffled. But, alas,
poor child! she had not been taught to keep
her evil temper under control. So she brooded
over Hugh's conduct. The more she thought
of it, the more chafed and angry she felt.

Guy helped Carrie and his sister put on their
skates. Jessie had never had a skate upon her
foot before. Carrie had learned to use them a
little the previous winter. Hence, she glided
off something like a swan, while Jessie hobbled
and slipped, and tumbled for a long time in vain
attempts to keep upright on the ice.

Carrie was so taken up watching the laugha-
ble attempts of her friend, that she took no

notice of poor Madge. Guy and Jessie were so busy, the former teaching, and the latter learning, that they too forgot her. Poor child ' this neglect stung the wound which Hugh's act had caused, and so, with many a frown and pout, she quietly stole from the hollow to a deeper one in which, by seating herself on a low stump, she could remain unseen.

"They is all proud," mused Madge, half aloud. " I heard that You, or Hugh, whatever they call him, say 'beggar's brat.' I know he meant me, and I know he went off cause I was with 'em. And there's them gals; they don't care for me a bit. Drat 'em ! I wish mother would go away from here."

This was very foolish talk for Madge. Had she looked on the kind side of her new-found friends, and thought of their gifts to her, and of the pleasant home they had given her and her mother for the time-being, and of their gentle words, she would have seen so much to be grateful for, that there would have been no room in her heart for unhappy feelings. But Madge forgot all these things. She saw nothing but

Hugh's scorn and Jessie's neglect. With these she tortured herself. It was just as foolish as if she had taken some sharp thorns and scratched her arms and cheeks with them.

While Madge was thus making herself miserable, Jessie was making rare progress with her skating. After a few awkward falls and a few bumps and bruises, she learned "*the how*," as Guy called it; and then, though still awkward, oh! how joyously she sped across the little pond chasing after Guy and Carrie, and shouting until the welkin rang again.

"Capital fun, isn't it?" said she, gliding ashore, and sitting down on a stone almost out of breath.

"I call it nice sport for girls," replied Carrie, pausing on the edge of the bank; "but you aren't tired yet, are you?"

"Yes, a little. Besides, too much of a good thing, as my uncle says, destroys your relish for it. I guess I've skated enough for once," said Jessie, stooping and unbuckling the straps of her skates.

"Pooh! Jessie's not half a skater!" rejoined

Carrie; "but what has become of your friend Madge."

"Sure enough! Where is she? I had for gotten all about her."

But Madge had wandered still farther off, and was nursing her bad feelings in a small grove which skirted the pasture. She was not visible from where the girls and Guy were.

"O Guy! Madge is gone. Won't you please come and help me find her?" said Jessie, putting on a very long and sorrowful face.

"I'll call her. She's not far off, I'll bet," replied Guy.

Then placing his hands to his lips as a sort of speaking trumpet, he shouted—

"Madge! Ma-adge! Ma-a-adge!"

"Adge! Adge! Adge!" said an echo from the distant grove.

"Where can she be!" cried Jessie, now relieved of her skates and standing on a hillock, peering eagerly all over the pasture.

"I guess she is only gone home. Never mind her," said Carrie. "She ain't worth worrying about."

" Yes, she is," replied Jessie. "She is a poor unhappy girl, and I want to make her good and happy. Uncle Morris says everybody that God made is worth caring about, and I *do* care for Madge. Oh dear, I wish I knew where to find her."

"See there?" cried Guy, pointing to a group of boys near the distant grove. "I think I see Madge among those fellows. I'll lose my guess if that isn't Idle Jem and his crew. There's a girl among them for certain, but how could Madge stroll all up there and none of us see or think of her ?"

" Let us go and see," said Jessie.

Quickly as their nimble fingers could loose the straps, Carrie and Guy removed their skates. In a minute or two more, the three were hurrying across the pasture toward the boys and girl, whom they saw

Madge was, indeed, one of that group. Idle Jem and his crew, while wandering across the pasture in search of the hickory-nuts which were hidden under the dead leaves, had found her in the grove. They began to jibe at her at once. The girl long used to the rough news and beggar boys of the city, and out of temper, withal, jibed back at them with interest. They goaded her with harsh words; and when Guy and the girls came within hearing, she was using language such as the pure-minded Jessie had never heard before.

"Hush, Madge!" said Guy, putting his hand on Madge's shoulder. "Don't swear! It's wicked to talk so. You go home with Jessie and Carrie, I'll take care of these boys."

That last phrase was an unlucky one for Guy. The wicked boys took it up as a defiance.

"Take care of us, eh? That's the talk is it? How will you do it, old fellow?" said Jem, sneering and chucking Guy's chin.

"Keep your hands off me, if you please," said Guy; "I want nothing of you only to let that poor girl alone."

"It's none of your business what we say to that gal," said Noll Crawford.

"Yes, it is my business to see that you let her entirely alone," replied Guy firmly.

"So stand off, and let us take her quietly away."

"Shan't do nothin' of the kind," said Peter Mink, running toward Madge, whose eyes flashed fire.

Guy grasped him by the collar and hurled him back from Madge, amidst the tears and cries of Carrie and Jessie who were both very much frightened.

"Oh! oh! a fight is it you want? Come I'll fight with ye!" said Idle Jem, slipping up to Guy, and raising his fists as if for a battle.

"I never fight!" replied Guy. "Besides, we have nothing to fight about. I only wish you to let my little friend, Madge, alone."

"She!" retorted Jem, "that swearing cat your friend, Master Guy Carlton Pooh! You don't have swearing gals among your friends, I know. That gal is some beggar's brat, and we only want to have some fun with her."

Jem's tone was much lowered toward the latter part of his speech. His hands, too, fell as if by instinct to his pockets. Peter Mink and

Noll Crawford drew back, the latter saying as
he did so—

"Come, Jem, let's leave the spunky little
gentleman and his friend, Madge, to themselves. I'd rather pick up hickory nuts than
listen to his gab."

"Discretion always is the better part of val-
or, as Uncle Morris says," thought Guy, as he
walked away with his sisters, patting the head
of old Rover.

It was the coming up of old Rover which had
cooled off Idle Jem and his crew. The dog
had been strolling about the pasture while
Jessie was skating. Having missed his young
master and mistress on returning to the pond,
the faithful fellow had followed them. He
came up just at the right moment. His rows
of big white teeth, and his low growl, taught
the idlers the discretion which Guy praised and
which led them to cease their angry jibes.
With Guy alone they might have contended.
But Rover was an enemy they had not courage
to face.

To the wounded pride and the ill temper of

Madge, shame was now added. The kind and gentle Jessie had heard her *swear*, had seen her face flushed with passion, had had a glimpse into the dark corner of her evil nature. Poor Madge! She sullenly refused to speak or to permit either of the party to take her hand; but lagging behind the rest, she silently followed them home.

Jessie bade her friend, Carrie, good-by in front of Mr. Sherwood's cottage. As they kissed each other, Carrie put her mouth to Jessie's ear and whispered—

"Jessie, shall I tell you what I think about Madge?"

"Yes."

"I wouldn't trouble my head about her any more, if I were you. She is a terribly wicked creature!"

Jessie sighed, but said nothing. On reaching home finding no one at liberty to talk with her, she went to her chamber and getting her writing materials and her portfolio, went down into the parlor and wrote the following answer to her cousin Emily's letter:

DEAR COUSIN:

I was glad to receive your letter, and to learn that you were all well at Morris-town. I cannot tell you how happy it made me to hear that you are trying to be good. I wish I was good all the time, but, as Uncle Morris says, it is so much easier to do wrong than it is to do right. I can't tell you how much I love our dear uncle, for he is always helping me to be good. He says a good heart is God's gift, and that we must ask him to give it to us for the sake of his dear Son. Well, I ask for a good heart three times every day, and if you do so too, God will hear you and bless you.

What do you think? Yesterday I found a poor girl named Madge in the road near the pump at the four corners. You know the place. Well, I asked Uncle Morris to take her home and he did. Her mother is here too. I thought Madge was so nice, and would learn to be good *so* easy, that I began to love her dearly. But to-day, she swore dreadfully and wouldn't speak to me. Isn't it fearful? I'm afraid I shan't be able to love her as I want to any more. Oh dear! I'm so sorry. Well, you and I must try to be good. Give my love to uncle and aunt, and to Charlie, and believe me to be

Your affectionate Cousin,

JESSIE CARLTON.

P. S. I've almost finished Uncle Morris's slippers. J. C.

# CHAPTER XIV.

"WELL, Jessie, how do you like your black-eyed *protégé?*" asked Uncle Morris, a few days after the events recorded in the last chapter.

"Pretty—well—but—but—"

"But what?" said Uncle Morris, with an arch glance, for he saw that Jessie was loth to speak the thought that lingered in her mind.

"Well, I like Madge, Uncle, but as ma says, she is not quite an *angel*," and Jessie laughed as if there was something funny in her mother's saying..

"I suppose she is not. Did my puss ever hear of angels being found, as we found Madge, dressed in rags, and shivering under a stone wall?"

"No, uncle, but, but—"

"There you are *but*-ing again," said Mr. Morris. "Why not out with it at once, and

14

say that you did not expect to find so many faults in poor Madge, as you have found?"

" Because I don't like to speak evil of her, and yet I do wish she wouldn't have those ugly spells come over her. Sometimes she is so gentle and grateful, that I begin to love her dearly. Then all at once, she will be so cross and ugly, that I begin to repent having asked you to bring her home with us."

Mr. Morris looked at his perplexed niece in silence for nearly a minute. He was thinking how to impress her mind with the moral taught by her disappointment respecting Madge. At last he very gravely said :

" Jessie !"

" What is it, Uncle?" asked Jessie, surprised at her uncle's manner.

" Shall I tell you plainly, why you *feel* so much disappointed in poor Madge?"

" Yes, Sir."

" Well, it is because your kindness to her was mixed with a good deal of *selfishness*."

" O Uncle-Morris!" exclaimed Jessie; " how can you say so?"

"Because I really think so;" replied Mr Morris.

"Well, you are a funny man, if you think so, Uncle! How *could* I be selfish, in wishing you to bring that poor child home? I'm sure I didn't expect to gain any thing by it." Here Jessie pouted a little, for she was really piqued by what her uncle had said. Seeing this, Mr. Morris replied:

"I hope my little puss is not going to be angry with her poor old uncle, because he seeks to tell her the truth."

"Well, no; but really, I don't see how you can think me selfish, just for wishing you to bring a poor, freezing child, to our house," and with this remark, Jessie forced back the smile which usually played round her lips, while she looked earnestly into her uncle's eyes.

"Will my little puss answer me a question or two?"

"Yes, Sir."

"Tell me then, my dear child, did you not expect to derive a great deal of *pleasure* from Madge's gratitude, and love, and obedience to

yourself? Did you not look upon yourself as
her benefactor, her teacher, her superior, and
as having a right to claim such conduct from
her, as would, in some degree, pay you for your
trouble and kindness? You expected her, poor
thing, to behave like an angel, for your sake.
Instead of that, she has, at times, let her evil
nature and her bad habits break out, in a way
to give you trouble and pain, and to cause you
to feel disappointment. Are not these things
so, my sweet little puss?"

"Yes, Sir. But—but *ought* not poor people
to be grateful and obedient to those who help
them?" asked Jessie, who, though she began to
perceive that a regard for her own pleasure had
been mixed with the kindness to Madge, was
not quite ready to plead guilty to her good
uncle's charge.

"They *ought* certainly, and when they do, it
is very right for those who help them, to take
pleasure in their gratitude. But that is a very
different thing, from doing good *for the sake of
the pleasure or profit we expect to derive from
the conduct of those we benefit.*"

Uncle Morris then went on to show Jessie, that really good people were kind to the poor and wretched, because it is their duty to be so; that they seldom found their reward, either in the gratitude of those they helped, or in the smiles of men; that instead of finding such rewards, they were often blamed and treated harshly by the public, and ungratefully by their *protégés;* but that they had a rich reward, nevertheless. They felt, he said, a very sweet satisfaction in themselves; they were smiled upon by the Father and Saviour of men; and they would, in the better land, be more than rewarded with mansions, robes, crowns, and honors, which selfish people would forever envy but never enjoy.

This talk with her uncle did Jessie good. She afterwards bore Madge's outbreaks of temper with more patience, and tried to set her such an example as would make her feel her own faults far more than by scolding or fretting.

Madge, who was very quick-witted, saw and felt the change in Jessie, and she, too, tried to overcome herself, that she might not grieve a friend, who loved her so truly and so well.

One morning Jessie awoke, and was surprised to see the lawn, the trees, and the fences all white with snow. It was a beautiful sight. She had never seen snow in the country before. Having dressed herself, she ran down-stairs, and going to the piazza, clapped her hands, and cried:

"Oh, how pretty those evergreens look! That pine-tree is perfectly beautiful!"

"Ah, Jessie, is that you?" said Guy, as he came round the winding path, plunging through the soft snow with his thick boots, and dragging his sled after him.

"Yes, I'm here," replied Jessie. "But where have *you* been with your sled before break-fast?"

"Been coasting, to be sure. There's a capital place in the lane that runs past Carrie Sherwood's cottage. We couldn't do much this morning but tread down the snow; but after breakfast, it will be fine. Will you go with me then, Jessie?"

"I should like to, ever so much, but—"

"But what?"

"Well, I must work all the morning. That's my rule, you know. I'll go with you in the afternoon, Guy."

"I don't want to tempt you to neglect a duty," replied Guy, knocking the snow off his boots, against the step of the piazza, as he spoke, "but really, I'm afraid the coasting won't be worth the heel of an old shoe, by the afternoon. You see, the sun is very bright, and the snow isn't apt to stay long, so early in the season."

"I'm sorry," said Jessie, looking very down-cast, "but I must give it up, I guess. You see, I've finished uncle's slippers, and have almost done his watch-pocket. I want to finish it ever so much before Thanksgiving, which is to-mor-row, you know."

"That's right, stick to it, Sister Jessie! I won't train in the little wizard's company, so I advise you to lose this coasting treat, if the snow does go, and thereby gain a victory for which Corporal Try would promote you if he knew it."

With these words, Guy kissed his sister, placed his sled in the back-hall, and went to the breakfast-room, to which he was shortly followed by Jessie.

At breakfast, the boys discussed the question of the weather, and the snow very earnestly. They wanted the snow to last, first, that they might enjoy the sport of coasting, and then, that they might have a sleigh ride.

" How I should like a sleigh-ride," exclaimed Jessie, with brightening eyes.

"Guess you won't have it just yet," said Hugh. " The sun will melt the snow from the roads before noon, I guess, and its too light and loose for good sleighing this morning."

" I'm sorry, for I do want to coast, and to ride in a sleigh, so much—ever so much," said Jessie, sighing, and looking very sober—foı her.

"Can't you *coast* this morning, with the boys?" inquired Mr. Carlton.

"We don't want her," said Hugh, snappishly. " Girls are always in the way when coasting is going on."

"Ill-natured as ever, I see, Master Hugh," observed Uncle Morris.

"I want her," said Guy, "and will take her this afternoon, if the snow don't melt."

Jessie looked at her brother with eyes that seemed to say, "What a dear, good brother you are!" Mr. Carlton asked:

"But why not take her this *morning*, Guy, before the snow melts?"

"Because she thinks it is not best to go, Sir," replied Guy.

"Ah! ah! Not best to go, eh? What's going on at home this morning, Jessie?" asked Mr. Carlton, looking at his daughter, whose face was now red with blushes.

"Because Corporal Try won't let her," replied Guy, laughing and coming to her help. "He has given her a task which he wishes done before Thanksgiving, and she means to do it, too, in spite of the little wizard, who sits perched on my sled, in yonder hall, and saying, 'Come, let's have a good time together, this morning.'"

"Bravo! If this was the proper place, I

would propose three cheers for Jessie Carlton, and her friend the Corporal," said Uncle Morris Then turning to Mrs. Carlton, he added, " By the way, sister, do you know that I expect to hear of a wedding before long?"

"Indeed! Who are going to be married now?"

"No less a personage than that pesky little dwarf, who has given my little puss so much trouble. I learn that he has popped the question to Miss Perseverance, and if nothing happens, they will soon be joined in wedlock, by Parson Good-Resolution."

Of course this quaint way of praising Jessie for her self-denial and self-conquest caused a good hearty laugh all round the table. Jessie's cheeks bloomed like roses, and her heart went pit-a-pat with joy-beats. A happier breakfast party could scarcely have been found that morning in or out of Duncanville.

To increase the flow of Jessie's delight, shortly after she had taken her seat in her own pretty little chair, her uncle entered the parlor with merriment in his eyes, and said:

"Sew away, my little puss. The north wind
is on your side, and in spite of the bright sun
will keep the snow from melting, so that you
may coast after dinner with Guy and your
friend Carrie, and take a sleigh-ride, too, at
three o'clock with a funny old gentleman named
Morris. What do you say to that my puss, eh?"

"I'm *so* glad, I don't know what to say,
Uncle. But, see here! (and Jessie held up a
purple velvet watch-bag, ornamented with steel
beads.) I shall have it all done by twelve
o'clock!"

"If the little wizard don't hinder," suggested
her uncle, laughing and looking roguishly at her.

"Well, he won't," said Jessie, shaking her
head. "He is too busy courting Miss Perseverance to trouble his head about me. Ha! ha!"

Mr. Morris laughed heartily at Jessie's ready
use of his quaint fancy about the little wizard.
He had no doubt about her firmness. But
shaking his finger at her he said, "Take care!
the little wizard is a cunning fellow, and knows
how to ensnare little misses who have tasks to
perform," and left the room.

Strong in purpose, and cheered by the hope of the afternoon's pleasure, Jessie worked with such vigor on her watch-pocket, that she had put on the last bead, sewed the last stitch, and trimmed off the last loose thread before the clock struck twelve. Then she felt happier far than any child ever did in the enjoyment of pleasures gained by the neglect of duty. She had conquered a difficulty, had won a victory. had done a duty—had she not a right to be happy?

I could almost wish myself a child again for the sake of tasting that fresh, perfect, unmixed delight which welled up from Jessie's heart on the afternoon of that clear December day. First came the play of coasting. Taking her on his sled—"The Never-say-die"—Guy drew her to the lane near Mr. Sherwood's cottage and amused her until the merry sleigh-bells caused her to turn round. Then she saw a splendid sleigh drawn by two noble horses, and driven by a man who, from the way he handled the whip and reins, seemed born to be a coachman. Her mother and Uncle Morris

GUY COASTING WITH JESSIE. Page 227.

were in the sleigh. She stepped in. Carrie and Guy followed. Having wrapped themselves up well in the buffalo robes, word was given to the driver, and away they dashed down the road.

Merrily jingled the dancing bells, swiftly trotted the lively horses, smoothly glided the steel-shod sleigh over the snowy pathway, passing houses, barns, and fields, as Guy said, with the speed almost of a steam-engine. On they went, mile after mile, drinking in health and spirits from the pure winter air and tasting that real enjoyment which is found in innocent pleasures only. No wicked amusement ever did or ever can yield such delight as Jessie and her friends tasted on that sleigh ride.

It was quite dark when they reached home again. They were a little chilled with their ride, but the glowing fire which burned so cheerfully in the parlor grate, soon restored them to warmth and comfort. The tea-table was made cheerful by Jessie's account of the sports and pleasures of the afternoon.

After tea Jessie took Guy into the kitchen.

and taking the watch-pocket from beneath her apron, said—

"Guy, I want you to go with me into Uncle Morris's chamber, and help me fix a hook .c hang this watch-pocket on. I want to give uncle a surprise."

Guy gave his consent. Going to the nail-box he selected a small brass hook, with a screw at the end, and a gimlet. Then taking a light, he went up-stairs with his sister. Jessie pointed to the spot, over his bed, which she thought the best place for the hook. Guy bored the hole, screwed in the hook, and hung the pocket by its loop of braid upon it. Jessie clapped her hands, and said—

"Isn't it pretty! Won't Uncle Morris be pleased! My *quilt* covers his bed. The *slippers* I made him are under his chair, and now my *watch-pocket* hangs over his bedstead. I'll get his chair-cushion done next, and then I guess he will allow that I'm fit to be a share in your Try Company. Ha! Ha! Ha!"

# CHAPTER XV.

## THANKSGIVING DAY.

THE next morning was mild and clear. A bright sun shone gloriously forth, and aided by light airs from the south, softened the snow and made every thing, but the walking, as pleasant as nature ever is on a December day. It was thanksgiving day, too—thanksgiving was appointed in December that year—and all the inmates of Glen Morris arose in high spirits, expecting to spend that festal day in calm and quiet enjoyment.

At the breakfast-table, Uncle Morris excited some surprise, by putting on a very grave countenance, and saying—

"Some persons must have entered my room, last night!"

"Entered your room!" exclaimed Mrs. Carlton, turning a little pale, and forgetting what

she was about, so far as to overflow the cup she
was filling with coffee.

"Did they steal any thing, Uncle?" asked
Hugh, in a voice made husky by the alarm he
felt at the idea of burglars having been in the
nouse.

"Mind, my dear, you are flooding the tea-
tray with coffee," said Mr. Carlton, pointing to
the overflow of coffee in front of his lady.

"Did you see them?" inquired Jessie, also
pale with alarm.

These questions were put so rapidly one after
the other, that Uncle Morris had no chance to
explain himself for a few moments. Silence,
however, followed Jessie's question. Then the
old gentleman relaxed his muscles, smiled, and
said—

"I neither saw nor heard the intruders; yet,
I found unquestionable marks of their having
oeen in my room. They even made a hole in
one of the walls! Yet, strange as it may
appear, they not only took nothing away, but,
on the contrary, they left one of the sweetest
little chamber ornaments behind them I ever

saw. Such burglars are welcome to enter my room every night!"

"O Uncle Morris! I know what you mean," said Jessie, laughing, and shaking her fore-finger at him.

Mr. Morris's last words and his changed man-ner, had, of course, relieved all parties of their alarm; though none but Guy and his sister knew precisely what he meant.

"I shouldn't wonder if you did. Even the bird knows where it finds food, much more should intruders know where they intruded," replied Uncle Morris.

Jessie then looked at her mother, and said—

"Ma, Uncle means me and Guy, by his intruders. We went into his room last night to hang his watch-pocket over his bedstead."

"But what about the hole in the wall, Jessie? Did you and Guy dig that?" asked Hugh.

"Ha, ha, ha! That's only Uncle Morris's fun. Guy bored a little hole with his gimblet, to screw in the hook which was meant to hang the pocket on; that's all," replied Jessie.

"No, that wasn't all, either," said Mr. Mor-

15

ris, "for my little puss left the cutest little velvet watch-pocket I ever saw, hanging on the hook. There was some witchery in it, too, for it kept me awake over an hour. It seemed to hop down on to my pillow, and buzz in my ear, saying, 'I am a love-gift. The little girl who made me, made your quilt, made your slippers, and is going to make you a cushion. A pesky little creature tried hard to hinder her from doing it, but her love for you was so strong, she drove him away. I don't think there is any other old gentleman in Duncanville, loved by either niece or daughter, half so well as you are loved by the little miss whose nimble fingers made me!' Talking thus, the pocket kept me from going to sleep, until I began to fancy that my Jessie must have put a fairy into it."

"O Uncle Morris!" cried Jessie, with a glowing face and a heart dancing to joy-beats, as it perceived the affection for her, which Uncle Morris only partly concealed under his quaint and fanciful way of speaking. She craved no higher reward, than these ex-pressions of his love for her.

After breakfast and family prayers were over, Mr. Morris turned to his niece, and said:

"Jessie!"

"Yes, Uncle."

"I am going to take a little walk, before I go to hear our minister's Thanksgiving sermon. Will you go?"

"Oh yes, yes, Uncle, I should like it ever so much."

During this conversation, Mrs. Carlton had been looking out at the window. The snow was dripping from the eaves, and from the trees. It looked soft and soggy in the path, and she feared the walking would be too sloppy for her daughter. So she said:

"It is hardly fit for Jessie to go out walking, Brother. The slosh will be over her sandals, and she will get wet feet."

"Do you think so, Ma? Well, I'm sorry. But if I only had a pair of rubber-boots, like Carrie Sherwood's, I could go in spite of the slosh. Never mind,"—here Jessie's sigh showed how disappointed she felt,—"never mind, uncle will have to take his walk alone."

Some misses would have fretted over such a disappointment as this. But Jessie seldom fretted. _She had too much good sense, and too much good nature to fret. Perhaps this was one reason why she was loved so well.

When Mrs. Carlton had expressed her view of the bad walking, Uncle Morris left the room, so that he did not hear all that Jessie said in reply. He now returned, bearing in his hands a good-sized parcel, neatly tied and addressed in his own handwriting, to "Miss Jessie Carl-ton." Giving it to his niece, he said:

"Open Sesame! Perhaps you may find a tal-isman within this parcel, which will incline your mamma to change her opinion about the fitness of your walking out with me this morning."

Jessie untied the string, and on opening her parcel, looked up with eyes full of pleasure, and exclaimed:

"A pair of rubber-boots!"

Then dropping the parcel, she ran to her uncle, and gave him, I don't know how many warm kisses. After this, she took up the boots, and looking at them admiringly, said: .

"Oh, how nice! Now I can go out in sloppy weather, can't I, Ma! What a dear good uncle you are! What made you think of buying me these boots?"

"What made my little puss think of making me a watch-pocket, eh?" replied Mr. Morris: "but come, try on your boots, and let us be going!"

Mrs. Carlton having no fears about the slosh now that Jessie's feet were "*booted*," instead of being "*sandalled*," gave her consent, and a few minutes later, Jessie was trotting along at the side of her uncle, in the road which led toward the village. A hired man followed them at a little distance, bearing a large basket well filled with mince-pies, and other Thanksgiving luxuries for the table. Mr. Morris was going to distribute them among certain poor families, to whom he had sent turkeys the day before. It was part of his religion to do what he could to enable the virtuous poor to share in the pleasures proper to Thanksgiving day.

The first cottage at which they called, was a

very small one, occupied by Mrs. Clifton and
her daughter Madge. Having received proofs
in letters from her early friends that her story
was, true, Uncle Morris had hired this cottage
for her, and aided by Mr. Carlton, and a few
other kind-hearted men and women in Duncanville, had furnished it, and put her in posses-
sion. Mrs. Carlton had interested the village
ladies in her case, and they had agreed to keep
her supplied with sewing. The poor woman,
cheered by voices of kindness, and by the
warm sympathies of her generous patrons, had
pledged herself, to abstain from the drinks
which had well nigh ruined her. She had been
in her new home for over a week, and was
getting along quite cheerily.

When Jessie and her uncle entered, Madge
shrunk behind her mother. Ever since the day
on which Jessie heard her swear, she had acted
as though conscious that there was something between herself and Jessie which kept them apart.
I suppose that something was shame on her own
part, and a dread of being made wicked by being
too intimate with her, on Jessie's part. But

whatever it was, Madge had felt uneasy in Jessie's presence from that time to the present.

"Well, Mrs. Clifton, how are you getting on?" asked Mr. Morris, after giving her a portion of the contents of the basket, carried by the hired man.

"Pretty well, Sir, I thank you: indeed, Sir, I owe every thing to you, Sir."

"No, not to me, my good woman, but to God and this child," said Mr. Morris, pointing to Jessie; "but for her, your Madge would have gone to the alms-house, and you, perhaps, would have been kept in prison. It was to please my niece, here, that I took Madge to our house."

"A thousand blessings upon the dear child, and upon yourself, too, Sir," replied the woman with tears in her eyes.

Jessie's heart sent up gushes of sweet feeling at the sight of Mrs. Clifton's gratitude. With some trouble she coaxed poor Madge to kiss her; after which she and her uncle left the house.

"It is more blessed to *give* than to *receive*," said Uncle Morris, as they walked through the soft snow to the next cottage.

Jessie dwelt upon that remark, saying to herself, as she silently trudged by her uncle's side—

"That is *so*, I really do believe. I always did like to *receive*, to have those I love *give* me something. But I really think I felt happier in *giving* Uncle Morris his watch-pocket, and in taking poor Madge home, than I did in *receiving* my skates, or rubber boots, or any thing else I ever had given to me. It's queer it should be so, but so it is. Yes, it *is* more blessed to *give* than to *receive*. I'll remember that as long as I live."

These musings were broken by their arrival at Mrs. Moneypenny's. Here they found poor Jack, Guy's *protégé*. He had arrived from the hospital the day before. His leg, though still sore and stiff, was healed. Long confinement had made his face thin and pale. But he was very glad to find himself at home again, and was very busy helping his mother get the tur key, sent the day before by Uncle Morris, ready for the oven.

Here again Jessie found grateful hearts. After some other remarks, the old lady said—

"That nephew of yours is a wonderful boy, Sir. There ain't another such boy in all Duncanville. Only think, Sir, how he, a gentleman's son, has milked and fed my cow, twice a day, ever since my Jack, there, was hurt! Why, Sir, we should all have been in the alms-house if it hadn't been for him. May the dear lad never know what trouble means!"

"I'd die for Guy Carlton, any day!" said Jack, his eyes glistening with grateful tears as he spoke.

"Rather strong language that, my lad!" observed Mr. Morris.

" Well, I would, Sir. He's been so good to my poor mother, I'd do any thing for him. I never knew such a boy as Guy Carlton," rejoined Jack, with a warmth that defied contradiction, if it did not carry conviction.

Having again drawn on the contents of the basket for the supply of Mrs. Moneypenny's table, they withdrew followed by a cloud of good wishes from the hearts and lips of Jack and his mother.

Thus from cottage to cottage they passed, like angels of mercy, making glad the hearts of the poor.

Returning from these visits to Glen Morris, they prepared for church, where they heard a most excellent sermon, on the duty of gratitude to God. Divine service over, they returned home, sat down at the plentiful table, and feasted on the good things which usually make up a thanksgiving dinner, in homes of wealth and comfort.

When the dessert was brought on, a little paper box was placed, by the servant, beside Guy's plate. His name was written upon it in the well-known handwriting of his uncle.

"What have you there, Guy?" inquired Hugh, who sat next to his brother.

"Perhaps it's a jack in the box!" suggested Mr. Carlton.

"A watch! A *gold* hunting-watch! Oh, what a beauty! Just what I've been wanting,"

exclaimed Guy, opening the box; " but what's
this writing ?"

On the inside of the case was this inscription :
" Presented to Guy Carlton in token of my admiration for his kindness to a poor widow in the
time of her distress.—Mr. Morris."

Guy blushed deeply as his brother read this
inscription. He was not aware that his uncle
knew about his kindness to the widow. But
the old gentleman had heard all about it from
the grateful woman's own lips. He now told
the story to the family. Mr. Carlton was delighted, and spoke words of approbation that
sank deep into Guy's heart, where they were
treasured up with more care than he would
have kept ingots of gold.

But there was a frown on Hugh's face. He
had no watch, and Guy now had two. Hence,
he felt envious. But before he had time to express himself, as he was about to do, Guy took
his old watch from his pocket and placing it in
Hugh's hand, said :

" There Hugh, I'll give you my old watch.
It's a capital time-keeper !"

"Thank you," replied Hugh, repressing his frown, and trying to look pleased.

" He don't deserve it," said Uncle Morris.

During this last act of Guy's, the servant placed a letter and another box—a *very* small one —beside Jessie's plate. Opening the letter, she read thus:

CITY OF SELF CONQUEST, December, 18—

DEAR MISS CARLTON:

Permit me to inform you that I have this day been wedded to Miss Perseverance by the Rev. Mr. Good-Resolution. With your permission, I and my bride will take up our abode with you at Glen Morris. I have taken a new name in part, and with my bride's help, I hope to *help* you more than I formerly *hindered* you, to keep the rules of the Try Company. The box contains a gift from a mutual friend, who wishes you to admit me, in my new estate, to your friendship and confidence.

Very truly yours,

RIGHT IMPULSE.

" Ah, Uncle Morris, you wrote that, I know

you did!" said Jessie, laughing, and looking very archly at her uncle.

"Well, maybe it is an old man's folly that did it. But Jessie, I trust you have now so far conquered yourself that henceforth 'your *impulses* will no longer be like little wizards tempting you astray, but that they will be guided by *right resolutions*, and carried out with *perseverance*. You will thus become a true member of the Try Company, and live both a good and a useful life."

Jessie now opened her box. Taking a bright little object from its velvet lining, she placed it on her finger, and holding it up, exclaimed:

"What a dear little thimble! Oh! isn't it pretty?"

It was a golden thimble with her name inscribed upon it. It came from her uncle, as a token of his approval of her many efforts to bring her impulses under the control of the law of duty.

"I hope," he said to her after receiving her caresses, "that your hardest struggles with your old enemy are over. But no doubt the little

fellow will sometimes try to separate himself
from his good resolutions and from his bride
Perseverance. When he does so, you will be in
danger again. But be brave! Be thoughtful!
Be prayeIful! Trust in the Great Teacher!
Try, and try again, and Uncle Morris will never
have need to blush for his niece, Jessie Carlton."

After dinner our young folks got up a grand
romp in the parlor. Their father and uncle
joined them, and the jocund hours passed so
swiftly, that the dusk stole upon them una-
wares.

"Dear me! How early it is dark to-night,"
said Jessie, as panting with excitement, she sat
down in her own little chair.

" Hours fly on eagle's wings, when people are
pleased and busy, as we have been this afternoon," observed Uncle Morris in reply; "but
hark! our door-bell rings! Somebody is coming in. Boys, put the chairs to rights!"

Before the disordered room could be made fit
for a reception, the servant opened the door,
and said:

"Mr. Carlton, will you please step to the door?"

Going to the door, Mr. Carlton found a man standing on the door-step with a letter in his hand. A carriage stood in front of the piazza. Bowing to Mr. Carlton, the man handed him the letter, and said :

"I have brought Miss Kate Carlton from New York, to stay with you, Sir. She is in the carriage. This letter will explain the reasons of her coming."

Though greatly surprised at the sudden appearance of his niece, Mr. Carlton did not stop, either to read the letter or ask questions, but went at once to the carriage, and offering his hand to his niece, said :

"I am happy to see you, my dear, at Glen Morris. Come into the house. John will see to your baggage."

Kate put her fingers into her uncle's hand, and with a mincing step, walked into the hall. Mr. Carlton asked the man who accompanied her, if he would remain all night.

"No, Sir. I thank you. I must return by

the last train, which will be here, as soon as ]
can get to the station. Good night, Sir!"

"Good night," replied Mr. Carlton.

When Kate was conducted to the parlor, she
was of course, greeted with looks and expres-
sions of great surprise. Jessie sprang to her
cousin, embracing her, and exclaiming :

"Why Kate Carlton, is that you ?"

Guy took her hand kindly, and said, "I am
glad to see you, Kate."

Hugh also gave her his hand, but his words
were not gracious. He said :

"What, *you* come here again, Kate Carlton !"

Uncle Morris kissed her, and spoke very
kindly to her. Somehow, his instincts told him
that her sudden coming to Glen Morris, was
caused by some unexpected evil.

Kate returned these greetings very stiffly
She had a cold nature, which did not readily
respond to the emotions of others. She was
tired, she said, and would like to be shown to
her room as soon as possible. Jessie according-
ly conducted her to Mrs. Carlton's room, who

was as much surprised to see her, as the others had been.

As soon as she left the parlor, Mr. Carlton, who had been reading the letter which came with her, placed his hand upon his forehead, looked very gravely at Mr. Morris, and said:

"Bad news! Bad news! My brother is a defaulter in the ——— Bank, of which he was president. He left the city last night, for parts unknown. His wife is half distracted, and has gone home to her father. She has sent Kate here."

"A sad case!" remarked Mr. Morris, sooth ingly. "But are you sure it is true."

"Too true, I doubt not. This letter is from my friend, Mr. Estal, a leading director in the bank. There can be no mistake. It is terrible. Had my brother lost all his property by honorable misfortune, or had he died as a good man dies, it would have been nothing to this. Now he is ruined and disgraced. Terrible! Terrible!"

Mr. Carlton groaned as he uttered these words. His anguish was painful to witness

16

His brother's crime pierced his heart. Happily he was able to weep, and thus relieve the violence of his feelings.

"It is terrible indeed," replied Uncle Morris. "But while we deplore his fall, let us be thankful that *our* honor is unstained by his crime. Let us also strive not to give way to useless grief, but let us spend our energies in efforts to break the fall of his unfortunate wife and child, whom he has dragged down with himself to poverty, if not to shame. If *you* will give Kate a home, I will see to her education, and will provide her with clothing."

"Spoken like your noble self!" rejoined Mr. Carlton. "Of course, she shall have a home, so long as I have one."

A free conversation, between all present, followed this remark, during which Mr. Carlton tried to make his sons feel, that the most absolute poverty if combined with integrity, is preferable to wealth allied with dishonesty, and that it is better to die a pauper's death, than to be guilty of a dishonorable act.

As for Jessie, her heart was swelling with

generous impulses, towards poor Kate. "I will be a sister to her," said she, in reply to a reference made by Guy, to Kate's bad behavior during her visit, the previous summer, "and will do my best to make her both happy and good!"

"Take care, Jessie!" said Guy, laughing. "Perhaps she will tempt the wizard to forsake his bride, and to take to his old pranks again. What will you do then?"

"I will try to keep on such good terms with Perseverance, his wife, as to prevent that," replied Jessie. "See if I don't?"

"Good! I'll request Corporal Try to place your name in his roll of honor," said Guy; "but the tea-bell rings, let us go to tea!"

----

## CONCLUDING NOTE.

JESSIE CARLTON will appear again in future volumes of the G. in Morris Stories, in which it will be seen whether her victory over the little wizard was temporary or lasting; and whether she fulfilled her purpose, to do her best to make Kate Carlton both happy and good.

www.ingramcontent.com/pod-product-compliance
Lightning Source LLC
Chambersburg PA
CBHW030807020726
47499CB00006B/1811